THE MERMAID WITH TWO TAILS

ISBN: 9798224245321

Book Cover and Map Illustration by Adrienne Mione

First Edition

11 10 9 8 7 6 5 4 3

Star of the Sea Novellas
Book One

THE MERMAID WITH TWO TAILS

ADRIENNE MIONE

Remar
Gorena
Koren
Teldor
The North Sea
The Nameless Isles
Maria's Village
The Eloran Current
The Azure Isle
The Alabaster Sea
Falareach
Falara
Capital City
City
Village
Forest
Mountains
Border
N
W
E
S

Contents

CHAPTER ONE

Scales and Seaweed

Maria's *heartbeat thundered in* her ears. The little patch of seaweed that she sheltered behind swayed this way and that, bowing to the whims of the ever shifting water. She tried to sway with it, grimacing every time an unexpected movement revealed a bit of her skin in the imperfect hiding spot. Still, it was better than the oddly shaped rock a few feet away.

She tried to catch a glimpse of her pursuer through the fickle plants. How long had she been hiding? Thirty minutes or so? In just a few minutes she would be in the clear.

She couldn't let herself get caught this time; the stakes were too high.

A flash of blue scales alerted Maria to her discovery mere seconds before a small form barreled into her, wrapping her in a grip that was disproportionately strong for the tiny arms that encircled her middle.

Found you! Andrea's giggle rippled through Maria's mind with the words.

Maria wriggled out of her sister's grasp and took off, pumping her tails as fast as she could to propel herself through the water. She couldn't out swim the young mermaid, not with her limitations, but it never stopped her from trying.

Trying and failing.

She hadn't even made it thirty feet before Andrea trapped her again, her shimmering blue scales standing out against Maria's pale stomach.

Maria groaned, pulling herself out of the girl's grasp once more. She tapped her magic, allowing her scales to cover her exposed skin. She had found through much trial and error that vivid green scales were not conducive to hiding in the murky brown seaweed that surrounded their village.

It occurred to Maria to wonder why she let her sister talk her into these games of hide and seek, considering she always lost.

Race you to the top! Andrea said, shooting upwards in the water only to immediately return when she realized that Maria hadn't followed her.

Aren't you coming? she asked. *You did say we could go sing on the surface if I won.*

The smug note in Andrea's voice amplified Maria's exasperation.

"If I recall correctly," Maria said aloud, her strong voice rippling effortlessly through the water, "the actual promise was 'we can sing together'. I said nothing about going to the surface."

Only after making the promise had Maria realized the girl's plan. She would have been impressed with how neatly she'd been bamboozled, if she were not so annoyed at having been tricked.

Andrea smirked. *Alas, with this human voice I can't sing below the water's surface,* she declared dramatically. *How would we sing together if we must stay trapped beneath the waves?*

"And I can't sing in the open air, so how are we singing together if we go to the surface?" Maria countered, pointing out the flaw in her sister's plan.

Andrea's expression didn't falter. If anything, she grew more smug. *And yet, you're going to keep your promise like you always do.*

Maria pursed her lips. "Father would have my hide if he knew I let you up there. You know how dangerous it is."

Andrea rolled her eyes. *There hasn't been a human in this area since Mama died. They don't even know we're down here.*

A familiar dull ache in Maria's chest accompanied the words. It had been nearly six years since their mother passed away, but every time she looked in the mirror she saw her mother's face. She had inherited the same emerald green eyes and flowing black hair. Andrea shared these features as well, but her wider nose and thinner mouth more resembled their father. Andrea must miss their mother too, but she was four years younger than Maria so the memories weren't as vivid.

There was an element of truth to her sister's objections, Maria supposed. They rarely saw boats this far from shore. But human sightings happened often enough to be a concern. Being half human wouldn't save either of them from a fisher's net and with how slow Maria was in the water, getting caught was a real possibility. She had the good sense to stay away from things she couldn't out swim.

Except for mischievous young girls, that is.

Maria sighed. It wasn't as if they didn't do this often. She weighed the risk of being caught against the chance to make her sister happy and the last bit of her resolve crumbled.

"Ten minutes," she said firmly.

Andrea squealed with delight, doing a little somersault in the water. *We haven't done this in ages!* she exclaimed, swimming towards the water's surface.

"I mean it, Andrea! We can't be up there long." Maria swam after her sister.

Andrea leapt from the water, creating a ripple across the surface as she came back down. Maria followed several seconds behind her.

When she was younger, Maria thought that having two tails would make her a faster swimmer. To her disappointment, as she grew older, her bottom half had grown to more resemble human legs; half the size of a mermaid tail and shamefully thin. Her scales helped to reduce friction in the water, which made it easier to outrun predators…

It was better than nothing.

Andrea splashed around. "I never get to talk aloud!" she hollered gleefully at the sky.

Maria laughed along with her sister; her voice an odd screeching sound now that the water's pressure didn't obstruct the force of her speech.

You find a new way to trick me up here at least once a month, she said, throwing water at Andrea. *It's a wonder you bother bringing me along! You could just come up here by yourself and save me the hassle.*

Andrea huffed. "What's the point of talking out loud if there's no one around to hear what you say? Besides, it's not my fault you inherited Father's voice instead of Mama's. I do think you got the better end of the deal, since I have to trick you up here while you can talk whenever you please."

And here I thought we came up here to sing, Maria drawled. *I suppose if you truly love the sound of your voice that much—*

Maria's teasing was cut short as Andrea twisted away from her, smacking the surface of the water with her tail.

Maria gave another screeching laugh as she shielded her face from the resulting splash.

Alright! Alright, I yield! she said through a torrent of high pitched giggles.

Andrea emerged with a smirk. She settled down, releasing her transformation and turning her bare face to the sun.

"It always feels better up here with skin," she said with a contented sigh. "Scales get itchy when they dry out."

Maria tapped into her magic, removing her scales from just her face and shoulders. She closed her eyes as all of her tension melted away. She loved her home under the waves, but the sun was warm in a way that the ocean never would be.

"Do you think Mama ever missed living on the surface?" Andrea wondered aloud.

Maria opened her eyes and blinked. *What prompted that question?*

Andrea wasn't looking at her. She watched the sky, as if the clouds might hold the answer to her question. "Well, I only have to hold onto my magic for some of my scales. Even that much is exhausting sometimes. I can't imagine maintaining a full body shift all the time."

Maria shrugged. *I always figured that human mages were stronger than halflings. Why else would it be so hard to make a real tail.*

Maria had tried for years to replicate a true mermaid tail with her shifting, but she had never even come close. She still practiced regularly. It was only a failure if she stopped trying.

Andrea frowned, fiddling with her hair. She looked like she wanted to say something but was still working up the courage to do so.

After a few moments she shook her head. "Let's go back."

Maria's brow furrowed. *Didn't you come up here to sing?*

Andrea ducked under the water. *It doesn't matter. Father's probably going to come looking for us any minute and you've got a big day tomorrow.*

Maria grimaced. "Don't remind me," she said, following Andrea in the direction of their village.

Andrea stopped short. *Why? I thought you liked Loran.*

"He's nice and I'm lucky to have him," Maria said tersely.

Andrea lifted an eyebrow.

Maria looked away, biting the inside of her cheek. "I'll be happier with him than I would be alone. Who else is going to propose to the two-tailed freak?" She forced a smirk onto her face, trying to lighten the conversation. "You're lucky your human half just keeps you from talking."

And forces me to use magic constantly, Andrea reminded her.

"And forces you to use magic constantly," Maria acknowledged. "I'm just saying, I got the shorter end of the stick when it comes to looks. Half of the older merfolk think I'm a demon and the younger merfolk all think I'm a freak. Loran at least talks to me."

Andrea watched Maria, her lips pursed. *That isn't a good enough reason to marry someone,* she said, stubbornly refusing to drop the subject. *If you don't like him, call the whole thing off.*

Maria sighed. "I like him. Honestly, I do. I'm just tired. Let's get home."

She swam ahead, pointedly ignoring the concern on her sister's face. It didn't really matter if she liked Loran or not; there were no other options. Who else would promise to spend the rest of their life with her? What was Maria supposed to do when Andrea grew up and got married? Or when their father passed away? Was she to be an old lady without anyone to keep her company, wasting away on the ocean floor?

Maria rolled her eyes at the melodramatic thought. She had already found her life-mate. Worrying about that now was a waste of energy. Loran would treat her well and—perhaps after a few years—he might even grow to love her.

CHAPTER TWO

The Betrothal Ceremony

Maria picked at her food. Her stomach churned, threatening to rebel if she dared to eat anything.

This is ridiculous, she thought to herself. *This is what you and Loran have been working towards for an entire month now.*

They had filled almost every free moment of the last few weeks with plans and preparations; practicing their speeches and discussing where they would live. She was fully prepared for the ceremony that would make it all official.

But that was part of the problem: it didn't feel real yet. Every day Maria waited for Loran to burst into laughter; to tell her that this was all part of some elaborate joke; to laugh at her foolishness and join the other merfolk in mocking her.

Loran wouldn't do that. He was the only friend she ever had and the only person outside of her family that wouldn't act like that. But knowing that didn't seem to help. It only gave rise to the opposite fear. What if everything happened exactly as planned? What if Loran married her as he promised? What if he didn't grow fond of her, instead growing old and bitter that he had wasted his life on a marriage made out of pity?

Could anyone really love her the way she was?

"Are you feeling alright, Maria?"

The concern in her father's voice pulled Maria from her whirling thoughts. He watched her from across the table, thick brows pulled low over his eyes with worry. His long hair had grown gray over the last few years. Though he still tried to hide how greatly the loss of their mother affected him, he couldn't hide that much. Blue scales rippled on his face, matching Andrea's in every way but the shade, which was much darker than the younger mermaid's.

Merfolk scales grew darker as one aged. Some of the oldest merfolk—those who were over a few centuries old—were so dark that you could no longer tell what color they had been in their youth. Her father's scales were a deep shade of sapphire blue.

"I'm fine," Maria replied. "I was just going over the words for tomorrow."

Her father smiled, his eyes crinkling at the corners. "My little girl, eighteen already!" he said, love and affection making his words warm and vibrant. "You have kept me in suspense this past month! Do tell me who the lucky boy is!"

Maria returned her gaze to her plate to hide a blush. Her father always thought her prettier and more popular than she was. Perhaps that was the role of fathers; to endlessly support their children, whether they deserved it or not.

Maria forced a smile onto her face for her father's benefit. "Loran has proposed to me, and I have accepted," she declared in the closest tone to 'happy' that she could manage.

The statement was met with awkward silence.

Maria's father shifted uncomfortably. "Ah. Loran…" he said slowly. "He's a nice boy."

Maria bit back a groan. "It's not like I'm spoiled for choice. Loran is the only one willing to put up with my tails the way they are."

Her father's features tightened. "Don't talk as if you're broken. My daughters are perfect just the way they are." His deep voice rumbled through the room, the water around them vibrating slightly with the force of it.

"Even though one of them can't hide as well as the other," Maria muttered, drawing a frown from Andrea as well.

Maria sighed, reining in her temper. It wouldn't do her any good to antagonize the only two people in the village that were willing to spend time with her, and it wasn't fair to Andrea to bring up things that neither of them had any control over.

"He'll be good to me, Father," she assured him. "You'll see."

Maybe if she said it often enough, she could convince herself of that as well.

Her father watched her for a moment before nodding his head. "That's all that matters," he told her, affection back in his voice. "You deserve a man who will treat you like a queen."

The final statement was too much. Maria excused herself from the table, seeking out her bed. She didn't want to be alone forever; Loran was her only choice.

He's a good choice, she corrected herself sternly. He had always included her, and he was never cruel or dismissive. She would be happy with him as her spouse.

She just had to find a way to convince him that he'll be happy as her's.

~ ~ * * * ~ ~

Maria didn't sleep a wink. Every time she closed her eyes, a different merman laughed at her folly. She could hear Loran's laughter from every mouth as he rejected her with a hundred different faces.

The ceremony is a formality, She kept reminding herself. *Just a meaningless tradition.*

Loran had a whole month to change his mind. He had asked for her hand and no one was likely to contest him for the 'honor'.

Maria arrived at the ceremony early. The natural platform made of sand and coral had been rimmed with rock to stabilize it for regular use. Fish darted in and out of the colorful coral, like fairy lights in a rainbow sea. The inner edge of the platform was rimmed with a second layer of stones, these ones made of obsidian and perfectly smooth. They caught the faint beams of sunlight that managed to make it through the water, shimmering and sparkling with reflections of the surrounding coral.

Maria's mood should have reflected the beautiful scene. Instead, her stomach twisted as she tried not to lose her breakfast.

Merfolk trickled in, forming a loose semi-circle around the platform. They probably only came out because the two-tailed freak was trying to find a husband and everyone wanted to see what unlucky soul had caught her eye.

Maria searched the crowd for Loran's sandy brown hair as her tension mounted. Surely, he wouldn't be late on such an important day. His nervous nature normally had the opposite effect. Loran showed up to most scheduled meetings a full hour before anyone else.

She was probably just too tired to pick him out of the crowd. She was already feeling the effects of her sleepless night.

"My daughter! My flower! The one who brings light to my life and laughter to my home," her father began, projecting his voice effortlessly to the edges of the small crowd that had gathered. His beaming face and crinkled eyes helped to turn Maria's apprehension into excitement.

This was really happening!

"The day has come when you leave my home to join another," her father continued. "but know that you will always be in my heart. Whenever you wish it, return to my home, and you will have a place at my table."

Tears pricked Maria's eyes. She blinked a few times to clear them.

"Now, who is the lucky man who shall claim your hand? I wish to see him for myself to know that he is worthy of you."

Maria grinned broadly, looking expectantly out at the crowd. This was the part where Loran would come forward and declare her his, challenging any man who wishes to steal her to a battle of wits or brawn.

Loran was likely to choose the first one if any challenger emerged, but Maria knew there wouldn't be one, so it didn't really matter. She waited patiently for him to build up the nerve, hoping he didn't stumble over the words they had practiced together.

Loran had been so nervous over the past week that he kept forgetting his lines. Maria had helped him learn it, even though it should have been easy since it was said at every betrothal ceremony. She had learned the speech by heart by the time she was five.

She recited the words in her head now, running out of things to keep her occupied as she waited for the timid boy to appear.

I, Loran, son of Teera, claim the hand of the Lady Maria. She has stolen my heart with her smile, and I give her my future to trade for it back. If any man should think him-

self more worthy of her affection, challenge me to a duel and I shall prove my right as her suitor. Should they win, I will step aside, for my lady's happiness is more important than my own.

Maria finished the speech three times. Then a fourth, for good measure. Loran would show himself any minute. He was not so cruel as to leave her floating there, alone and embarrassed…

The crowd shifted awkwardly. Loran did not appear.

As the minutes stretched on, Maria's smile faded, and her cheeks burned scarlet.

One by one, the merfolk lost interest and swam away. A few of the older merfolk offered an encouraging word, telling her that she would find a nice boy; she just had to be patient.

Maria gave a polite nod as they left, not trusting her voice.

She was left on the platform, alone except for her father and her sister: the only two people in the world who cared about her.

CHAPTER THREE

The Cove

*M*aria... ***Andrea put a*** hand on her shoulder.

Maria shrugged her off, swimming away from the platform as fast as her tails could take her. She swam past homes and coral gardens, ignoring the pity of the older merfolk and the taunting of the young. Tears of embarrassment and anger spilled into the sea as she swam.

She headed straight to the seaweed patch where she knew she would find him, and sure enough, she spotted Loran's murky brown scales cowering behind a large rock.

"Why weren't you there?" Maria demanded, drawing a startled look from Loran who hadn't seen her approach. She glared at him as he squirmed.

"Maria! I-I—" he stuttered.

"You asked me to marry you a month ago," she reminded him, her fin-like ears flaring outward with her displeasure. "You were supposed to formally ask for my hand. How could you forget to show up and embarrass me in front of the whole village?"

Loran shrunk a little further behind his rock, seeking shelter from her anger. "I didn't forget," he admitted.

Maria's heart dropped, her anger fading away as her ears returned to their normal place at the side of her head. She sank a few inches in the water as the reality of the situation hit her.

"You changed your mind." She didn't phrase it as a question.

Loran dropped his head in shame.

"I promise I won't give up." Maria couldn't keep the desperation out of her voice. She wouldn't let go of her only chance at happiness so easily. "I'll figure out the shift. I'll have a normal tail. Just put up with me for a few years. I'm getting so close."

Loran shook his head, his eyes wide. "It's not that!" he said quickly. "I talked to my parents last night. I told them I planned to ask for your hand. My mother was livid. She told me that I should choose a proper mermaid to marry. She said we wouldn't be welcome in her home or at her table. I tried to talk her around, I really did…" He gave Maria a helpless look.

Her gut twisted as her nightmares played out before her eyes.

Loran didn't want her. He wasn't even willing to fight for her. Why should he? What gave her the right to rip him from his family's arms? Was she so selfish that she truly wished to steal his heart from him, so that his only choice would be to trade his future to get it back?

Her only choice, her last resort, the one she thought she could live with despite his lack of true affection for her, Loran had withdrawn his proposal. Maria was to be alone—truly alone—for the rest of her life.

She closed her eyes and shook her head. "Don't come to see me anymore," she told him. "I don't know if I can handle seeing your face right now."

Loran moved toward Maria, but she swam away, not caring which direction she went as long as it took her away from him and the future she could no longer have.

She'd been swimming for nearly half an hour when Andrea caught up with her.

Maria! her sister called from behind her. *Maria, wait!*

Maria laughed harshly. "Why?" she yelled back at Andrea. "You'll catch up to me soon enough."

Andrea growled telepathically before doing just that. Passing Maria, she grabbed her arm and started pulling her in a different direction.

"Where are you going?" Maria asked, irritation filling her voice. She tried to pull free from Andrea's grasp.

I need to show you something, the younger mermaid said, holding her firmly as she dragged Maria even further from the village.

Maria sighed. "Can't it wait? I don't really feel like playing right now."

Andrea shook her head. *It can't wait.*

Her sister offered no more explanation.

Maria frowned but didn't argue. It wasn't as if she could resist if her sister was set on dragging her somewhere. Andrea's tail was far stronger than hers.

All she wanted was her bed. Or maybe a hole to hide in until everyone forgot she existed. Why had she ever believed she could get married? She should have aimed lower; tried to become a nanny for the children. It's not like a tail was required for babies that could hardly swim.

The water grew shallower as they swam. Her feet started to brush the bottom of the ocean and it took effort to keep her head in the water.

"Why are we heading toward land?" Maria narrowed her eyes at her sister, wondering what her intentions were with this impromptu adventure. Andrea turned to look at Maria, a broad grin replacing her serious expression.

You'll see in a minute! she said cryptically.

Andrea dragged her all the way to the beach, settling

into a sitting position and turning to Maria. The waves pushed and pulled at Maria as she examined her sister for some hint as to what it was she was supposed to be seeing.

Andrea looked away and played with the sand around her tail, the hesitation she had displayed the previous day returning once more to her features.

Well? Maria prompted, unable to stand the awkward silence a moment longer.

Andrea stopped messing with the sand and took a deep breath. "I've been practicing with my magic and I wanted to find the perfect time to show you. But you had so much on your mind, and I didn't want to add to your stress and then there was the disaster today with Loran and Father said you needed time and–"

Maria grabbed Andrea's arms to stop the torrent of words. *Show me what?* she prompted again.

A slow grin spread across Andrea's face as she moved closer to shore, her tail emerging from the water.

Only Andrea no longer had a tail. Instead, she had two human legs. They were perfectly formed with bright pink skin and short stubby toes. She shifted her top half as well, getting rid of her scales and rounding off her ears to more resemble a human's features.

Maria's mouth hung open and she crawled forward to grab one of her sister's legs and examine it.

"You shifted? As in a full shift into a human?" In her shock and amazement, Maria had forgotten to use telepathy. Her screeching voice echoed around the empty cove, sending birds flying in the forest beyond.

Andrea cringed. "Fully human, ears and all," she said ruefully.

Sorry, Maria said, shifting herself human and taking a seat next to her sister. She smiled as she wiggled her toes in the sand, marveling at the sight they must make. There they were, two young women, sitting out in a cove on a deserted island. Maria closed her eyes and tilted her head back, letting the warmth of the sun wash over her.

Wait, how did you manage this? she asked, turning back to look at her sister. *I thought you couldn't do the bottom half.*

Andrea chuckled. "It took me months to get the feet right. You use your human form when we play hide and seek, so I used that as my reference point for how to shift."

Maria shook her head. *Once again, you prove yourself far too cunning for your own good.*

Andrea tilted her head playfully. "One of us had to be. You're far too fond of rules for my liking." She sat up straight. "Come on! I want to go explore the forest!"

Maria's eyebrows climbed to the top of her forehead. *Are you insane? What are we supposed to do, drag ourselves along on our stomachs?*

Andrea laughed. "I've been working on that, too!" She placed both hands on the ground and shakily rose to her feet. She wobbled for a moment before regaining her balance.

Grinning broadly, she lifted a foot and placed it on the ground in front of her. She did it again, and again, until she was confidently striding across the beach.

Maria narrowed her eyes. *Just how many times have you come up here?*

Andrea shrugged. "I couldn't practice walking in the water," she said. "Remember how Mama used to bring us here every now and then to shift? She would tell us all those stories about what the surface world was like and how she'd sailed across the ocean on a mighty boat!"

Maria smiled. *I don't think this is the same cove,* she told her sister. *But I remember. I also remember her telling us that it was too dangerous to go near humans, no matter how beautiful the surface might be.*

Andrea waved a hand dismissively. "The island is deserted. We're not going near humans; we're just learning to walk! I remember vaguely how Mama used to do it, but I think my posture is weird. Either way, it works! You should try it!"

Maria hesitated, biting the inside of her lip as she eyed the uneven sand. Before she could come up with an excuse, Andrea was beside her and pulling on her arm to help her stand. Maria let out a yelp of protest, struggling to get her feet under her. Andrea didn't let go until she found her footing.

Maria wobbled, feeling as if her legs were carrying far more weight than they must have been. Slowly, with her arms stretched out to either side for balance, Maria picked up her left foot and placed it on the ground in front of her. The wet sand sank slightly under Maria's weight, and she fell to the side.

She threw her other foot out wide to catch herself. Andrea pushed hard against Maria's left side, holding her upright as best she could as Maria regained her balance. The two girls made their way haltingly onto the beach, gaining confidence with every step.

Excitement bubbled in Maria's chest. She hopped around on the hot beach, taking great delight in the way the sand splashed whenever she jumped.

Picking up her foot, she examined it curiously. *Why is the sand so sticky?*

Andrea giggled. "I think it's because of the water," she replied. "If you wait until your feet are dry it stops sticking to you."

Maria shook her head. *I knew you were crazy, but spending enough time up here to dry out? How have you never been caught?*

Andrea took a few steps further onto the beach and spun around happily, her arms outstretched.

"Because there's no one out here!" she exclaimed. "I

told you, it's a deserted island! What are you afraid of?"

Maria shook her head again. *I'm sure there are land animals in that forest behind you. They seem plenty scary to me.*

"You have no sense of adventure." Turning, she bounded off into the forest, leaving Maria alone on the beach.

CHAPTER FOUR

Not-So-Deserted Island

*A*ndrea! *Wait!* **Maria took** off after her, stumbling often as she tried to figure out how to use longer strides. She ran into tree roots and low branches in the dense forest, leaving painful spots that would probably be bruises the next day. She tried to keep Andrea in sight as she ran.

Come on, Maria! Andrea called back telepathically. *You can't be slower than me in water* and *on land!*

Despite herself, a wide grin spread across Maria's face. *You'd better not let me catch you! I have fourteen years of mermaid hugs to make up for!*

Andrea's laughter rippled through the air and Maria sped up, catching her stride in what she hoped was a natural enough run. She wasn't entirely sure what to do with her arms so she held them out a few inches from her waist, ready to steady herself if she lost her balance. Wind blew past her, roaring around her ears like the crashing sound of waves. Her heart raced, adrenaline chasing away her earlier fatigue.

She caught up to Andrea and dragged her backwards into a giant hug, accidentally lifting her off the ground with the force of her affection. The younger girl let out a peal of laughter, and Maria joined in. Their voices ringing clear and pleasant in the empty forest.

Maria froze as Andrea pulled out of her grasp.

"You shifted your voice box?" Andrea asked incredulously.

Maria placed a hand on her throat. The laugh had sounded natural; no screeching or high pitched quality to it at all.

"I can talk?" she asked aloud.

Andrea winced. "Not quite," she said. "It still sounds like you swallowed a dolphin. You'd better stick to telepathy."

Maria couldn't hide her disappointment. She thought she had finally accomplished something beyond her normal shift pattern.

Andrea nudged her with her shoulder. "At least you can laugh. That's more than I can do in the water."

Maria's mood lifted. *That's true.*

"Let's keep exploring! Maybe the fresh air will help you shift the rest of the way."

They took off in the direction they had been running. Maria ran just ahead of Andrea, delighting in the fact that she could outpace her younger sister for the first time in her life.

The forest grew denser as they ran, forcing them to slow their pace as they navigated tree roots and bushes. The vivid green of the trees mixed pleasantly with the colorful flowers that grew unchecked in the vibrant landscape. Small animals scurried away as they passed and birds took flight, chirping their objection to this intrusion on their solitude.

Maria stopped, doubling over as she gulped for air.

Running takes a lot more effort than swimming, she said, clutching her side.

Andrea laughed breathlessly. "That's true. I don't think I've ever run that much." She paused every few words to draw in a quick breath.

Maria opened her mouth to say something else, but a rustle of movement behind Andrea caught her eye.

She straightened, squinting into the dense forest as she moved to stand beside her sister. *Did you see–*

Two large men burst out of the thicket of trees, grabbing the two girls and throwing them over their shoulders. Maria screamed, beating her fists on her attacker's back as she tried to wriggle out of his grasp. Andrea yelled various colorful insults at her captor, scraping her claws across his back as she struggled.

"Let me go!" Maria yelled, her terror making her lose part of the shift. Her voice came out as an ear shattering screech and the men looked at each other with startled expressions.

"You got yourself a screechy one there, Renner," the man holding Andrea remarked.

Renner adjusted his grip on Maria, her middle colliding painfully against his broad shoulder. "Should we knock her out? My ears are ringing from that last scream."

The other man shrugged. "Probably'd be better. The one I grabbed's got some claws on her and I'm not looking for a back scratch."

Renner dropped Maria, the hard earth knocking all of the air out of her lungs. She struggled to breathe as she looked around wildly for Andrea. Her sister lay a few feet away, gasping for air as a giant of a man towered over her, a rock raised and ready to strike.

Andrea!

Maria felt a sharp pain on the back of her head and the world went black.

~ ~ * * * ~ ~

Shouting echoed around Maria. She groaned, the sound coming out higher than it should have. She quickly checked her shifting to make sure she was still human. Only her voice had slipped. She fixed it as best she could and cracked her eyes open.

She squeezed them shut again as the bright sunlight assaulted her senses, inspiring a wave of nausea in Maria's stomach.

"Not only did you bring me unknown wares only a few days before we sail to market," a gruff female voice said. "but you damaged the goods with your idiotic attempt to keep them quiet. I should throw you overboard and let you explain yourselves to the sharks."

"You shoulda heard 'em Captain. It was like a screech owl. My brains are still jostlin' about in my noggin." Maria couldn't place the second voice but it sounded familiar.

Where were they, exactly? They had been in the forest. Maria remembered the pretty flowers and some trees. They had been exploring. Why was her head so fuzzy?

Maria sat bolt upright as the events of the afternoon came back to her in a rush. The fast movement sent pain lancing through her temples. She tried to back away from the group of unfamiliar faces but wooden bars stopped her escape.

Andrea groaned at her side. Crawling forward, Maria placed herself between Andrea and the humans.

The woman—the Captain, presumably—was tall, with long red hair that seemed to glow in the sunlight. She had her hands on her hips, a scowl twisting her otherwise pleasant features.

"She's a tough one if she can think through that bump on her head. How many times did you hit her?"

Two men stood next to the Captain, one on either side. They were built like whales, with identical wide shoulders and heavy guts. The one on the Captain's right answered her question.

"She kept waking up," he told her. "I don't think it did any real harm. She may be a bit dull from here on out, but it's not like she'll be needing brains now."

The Captain rolled her eyes. "It would make my job easier if you had some brains of your own."

"Renner's plenty smart, Captain," the other man objected. His one distinguishing feature from Renner was a patch over his right eye. "Ma always said he got the brains in the family."

"Unfortunately, it seems there wasn't much to inherit," the Captain responded dryly.

Renner and the other man both looked confused, and the Captain rolled her eyes.

"Never mind. Where did their clothes go?" She wrinkled her nose. "And why do they smell like you fished them out of the ocean."

"That's how we found 'em," the second man responded. "They's runnin' around the island in nothin' but skin."

The Captain frowned in distaste. "Find some sacks or something to throw over them and put the healer on those bumps. I won't be showing up to Teldor market with damaged merchandise."

The woman walked away.

Maria watched the two men warily, keeping a protective hand on Andrea's shoulder.

Her sister stirred. *What happened?*

Maria tightened her grip in warning.

Andrea froze. *What is it?*

We're in trouble. Keep quiet for now. I'm trying to find a way to get us out of this.

Renner turned to the second man. "Well, Patch, should we just bring the box with them?"

Patch rubbed the back of his neck. "I dunno," he said, gesturing at Andrea. "I don't wanna go up against that one's nails again."

Maria moved further in front of her sister, baring her teeth.

Renner backed up a step. "That one ain't right in the head. I think we'd best keep our distance if we don't want to catch some disease or something."

Patch's voice rose in pitch, "What if we brought the healer here? Then we can leave 'em up here and keep our fingers well away."

Renner nodded emphatically. "That's a good plan. You go get the healer. I'll watch the cage."

CHAPTER FIVE
The Grumpy Walrus

P_atch jogged to the_ other side of the boat, his heavy footsteps making a loud thumping sound against the ship's wooden floor.

Maria ignored him as he left, taking a look at her surroundings. There had to be a way to escape.

The sides of the boat didn't look too tall to climb over; the problem was getting there. Two men stood by a strange wooden pole that climbed into the sky. Large rectangles of cloth billowed in the wind…

What had her mother called them again?

Maria shook her head, immediately regretting it as her splitting headache intensified. The different parts of the boat weren't important. She had to get her and Andrea back into the water. She hoped this would be the only time she ever found herself on one of these wooden death traps. She'd seen enough wreckage from ships to know how often they sank.

What if they sank the boat? Then they could just swim away as the humans drowned.

But Maria didn't know how to sink a boat.

Maria put a hand to her head, struggling to think through the fog in her brain. She felt something wet, withdrawing her hand to find it stained red.

That's not good.

Patch returned with a short, stout man. His long mustache hung down either side of his face, reminding Maria of a walrus. She chuckled at the mental picture.

Maria frowned. Now was not the time to be chuckling; Now was the time to be escaping.

The walrus man approached with a sour expression on his face. "I have enough problems patching you pirates up without you bringing other things in for me to fix," he complained. "Keep the girl still. I'll have to make contact to heal her."

The two men hesitated.

"Maybe we could knock 'em out again and you could work on 'em when they're all quiet like," Patch suggested.

The healer pinched the bridge of his nose, a crease appearing between his brows. "It's that sort of boorish behavior that creates a need for my services." He waved a hand toward the door that led below deck. "Forget it, go find yourself some food and come back in an hour. I'm sure I can get them to cooperate better without you here anyway."

Renner glanced sidelong at the cage. "They're not ones you want to mess with," he told the healer. "They're not right in the head."

"Nor would you be if you had such a lovely collection of dents in your useless scull. Go now or explain to the Captain why I refused to fix her merchandise."

The healer crossed his arms, glaring up at the larger man. Somehow, despite being half Renner's height, he still managed to look intimidating.

Renner shrugged. "Its on you, I guess. C'mon Patch, lets go see if Alba's got any of that fish stew left from last night." His voice faded as the two men disappeared into the belly of the boat.

The healer turned to Maria and frowned. "Are you going to let me heal you or do I have to find a creative way to keep you still?"

Maria narrowed her eyes, watching the man's hand as he reached into the cage. He seemed different from Patch and Renner. At the very least he was funny looking. Pain flared in her head as his hand made contact with her injuries. She yelped, pulling away.

"Hold still," the healer grumbled. "It's going to hurt but it will hurt less if you don't prolong the process."

Maria approached slowly, bracing herself for another wave of pain. He moved forward and pressed his hand against her head. She grit her teeth, inhaling sharply, but this time she didn't pull away.

The pain faded after a few moments and Maria backed away as the healer removed his hand.

Maria breathed rapidly as her heart began to race. With her head clear, the bleakness of their situation hit her full force. Sweat dripped down her forehead as she felt around the cage for a way out.

The healer reached towards Andrea. Maria swatted his hand away, growling as she pushed Andrea backwards and away from the man. She gasped for air, trying to regain her equilibrium.

The man shook his hand out. "Lot of thanks I get for saving your life," he said dryly. "The names Gray, by the way. I know you're panicking but you better let me look at the little one if you don't want to find yourself alone on this rotten ship."

Maria closed her eyes and forced herself to take slow deep breaths. She walked herself through the situation as calmly as she could.

They had been captured by humans. The big ones,

Patch and Renner, were dumb and violent. She had been injured repeatedly. The healer, Gray, had fixed her.

Andrea needed to be fixed too.

Maria opened her eyes and kept her gaze fixed on the healer as she carefully moved out of the way so he could tend her sister.

Gray put his hand to the angry red bump that had grown on Andrea's temple. Maria flinched when her sister let out a pained whimper. The healer's hand glowed and the bump shrank, disappearing altogether in the space of a few breaths.

"There," Gray said, "Good as new. I wager we have some time before the grunts get back, so why don't you tell me a bit about yourselves while we wait."

Maria narrowed her eyes, returning to her position between Andrea and the healer. It didn't matter if the man was hostile or not, the less these people knew about them, the better.

Gray's sour expression returned and he huffed. "Fine, suit yourself. I was just bored anyway."

He stood up and walked away, leaving Andrea and Maria alone except for two sailors that were working by the mast on the far side of the ship.

What do we do? Andrea asked. She watched Maria with wide eyes, clearly expecting her to have all the answers.

What did they need to do first?

We need to get out of this cage, Maria told her, darting a glance at the other side of the ship. *Stand between me and those men and I'll get the door.*

Andrea stood up, blocking the men's view of Maria as she examined the rope on the cage. It didn't seem particularly thick. Carefully, she shifted her nails back into claws and sawed through rope. It gave easily and she shifted back as she held the door closed.

Checking to make sure that the men were preoccupied she turned to Andrea. *We need to get to the water. Follow slowly. We don't want to draw their attention.*

Andrea swallowed hard and nodded. They eased the door open, slipping out of the cage. They crept silently over to the side of the ship.

Maria grabbed the railing just as a large meaty hand grabbed her from behind and threw her across the deck.

"Gray said you was finished, but I didn't expect you to get outta your cage," Patch remarked, grudging respect in his voice.

Andrea struggled against Renner's grasp on her arm as Maria scrambled away from Patch.

He towered over her, blocking the sun as a sneer spread across his face. "Should we have some fun with 'em?"

The words sent a shiver down Maria's spine.

Renner snorted. "Little thing like that's not gonna be much fun, anyhow. let's just put 'em with the others."

CHAPTER SIX

The Farmer from Falara

Renner shoved Maria into a small room below deck. She fell face first onto the wooden floor, letting out a pained cry as Andrea landed on top of her. The overwhelming odor of dirty bodies mixed with the foul odor of the garment that Renner had thrown over Maria's head.

She gagged, running to the corner as she lost the contents of her stomach. She spit, trying to clear her mouth of the rancid taste before turning to examine their surroundings.

Maria had to shift her eyes back to normal to see anything in the dimly lit room. A single lantern hung from a hook in the middle of the ceiling, casting it's weak light on the group of humans huddled together in the opposite corner. They watched her warily, squinting to try to see her with their weaker night vision.

Maria drew away from them. Putting herself between Andrea and the humans, she positioned their backs against the far wall for security.

She counted ten people. They varied in age from a small child to a silver haired elder, but most of them were somewhere in the middle. Hollow cheeks and deep bags under their eyes told of many nights sleeping in this cramped cell.

Maria could easily defend herself from any of these people, but she was at a severe disadvantage. She had dubious control of her legs, and one slip up magically could leave her covered in scales.

A man—the only one who seemed relatively healthy—approached them from the group of captives. Maria tensed, pushing Andrea further behind her back.

The man held his hands up in a placating gesture. "You've got nothing to fear from the folks in this here room," the man told her. His accent differed from the other people she had met on the boat. It was softer and didn't lean as heavily into the consonants. "I won't lie and say everything is dandy, but no one in here'll hurt ya."

The man leaned to the side, trying to get a better look at Andrea. Maria shifted to better block his view and glared at him, baring her teeth threateningly.

He returned to his original position; his hands still raised as if to calm her.

"How about we start with some introductions," he suggested, taking a seat and resting his hands comfortably on his knees. "I'm Correll. I'm from a country called Falara." He lifted his hand and extended it toward Maria with an expectant look.

Maria frowned. She looked from the man's face to the proffered limb. What did he expect her to do?

Correll held his hand out awkwardly for a few moments before he retracted it, reaching up to scratch the back of his neck.

"You folks don't use handshakes, I see." He chuckled nervously. "You're from an island, right? Well, a handshake is something mainlanders do when they introduce themselves. I'm a farmer from a little town out in the boonies; I won't bore you with the name. Susanoo snatched me on my way to Gorena. She grabbed me and a few of my companions while we were docked for supplies. Didn't even see her coming. Anyway I was just trying to get to the port, you see…"

Maria relaxed slightly as he rambled on. In a way, this man reminded her a lot of Loran. The thought should have upset her, but in the face of everything that had happened since that morning, Maria couldn't seem to muster up the proper anger at her betrothed. Even if she didn't plan on trusting Correll, it was nice to have a little bit of familiarity in the midst of the nightmare she had found herself in. There was something about his cheer, however forced and awkward it may be, that made Maria want to sit and listen to him talk.

"…never been to Gorena's capital. Was going to visit distant family, you see, and well… I'm not exactly adept at protecting myself. I'm planning on escaping as soon as I'm able, but I suppose if it were that easy then slaves wouldn't exist in the first place, now would they?"

Maria's ease died instantly.

Andrea squeezed closer to Maria's back. "Slaves?" she breathed, her voice quivering.

The man's eyes widened. "You didn't know this was a slaver's ship? I thought it'd be obvious by the cages and bars and whatnot."

Maria looked around, seeing the chains that hung from the wall for the first time. The dim light from the lantern reflected off of the tarnished metal. The humans huddled together, watching the exchange with grim expressions. Maria took in their old and threadbare clothing. If this was a slaver's ship…

Maria stood, dragging Andrea toward the door. She grabbed the handle and pulled on it frantically as if she could rip the door off its hinges through sheer force of will. Andrea assisted in the effort, but the door didn't even tremble at their weak attempts.

This couldn't be happening. This could not be happening. They needed to get off this boat. They needed to get back to their village. She would not die on a filthy pirate ship. Something brushed up against Maria's arm and she lashed out, raking her nails across skin.

Correll backed away, eyes wide as he clutched his bloodied cheek.

Maria glanced down at her hand. Her bright green scales glinted in the dim light of the lantern and her fingernails were sharpened to their usual vicious looking claws.

She hissed, the sound coming out like a high pitched whistle in the open air. Closing her eyes, Maria took a deep breath, willing her magic to return her to her human form. She peeked on eye open and exhaled. The man's gasp drew her gaze. Panic rose in her chest but the intense look in his eyes made her pause.

"Show that to no one," Correll told her in an urgent whisper. "Not even the other slaves. You're lucky the light is so dim in here."

Maria's gaze darted to the other captives. They squinted through the darkness at her, able to tell that something had happened, but unable to witness what it had been. They looked merely curious, not frightened or even surprised. Maria turned her attention back to the intense farmer.

"Why?" Andrea asked in a shaky voice.

The man turned to her. "Gorena is not kind to their mages. You're better off sold as a slave than burnt at the stake. Even in an escape attempt, it would be too risky to use magic."

"Burnt?" Andrea squeaked, eyes bulging.

Stop talking. Maria shot her sister a stern look. *We don't know him, and you don't even know what burnt at the stake means.*

Whatever it is, it doesn't sound good, Andrea countered. *He's the only one who seems to be willing to give us any information. How are we supposed to pass for human if we don't know anything.*

Correll smacked Maria on the side of her head and Andrea let out a cry of protest.

Maria stared at him incredulously. *What was that for?*

"Don't do that either," he hissed. "Telepathy is a mage skill. It will get you caught."

Maria sank to the hard wooden floor. She wasn't even allowed to talk? How would she communicate? How was she going to protect Andrea? She buried her face in her hands.

Andrea sank down next to Maria, wrapping her in a tight hug. "We'll figure this out," she whispered. "We'll get out of this somehow."

~ ~ * * * ~ ~

Patch and Renner returned not long after. The captives rushed forward, eyes glued to the pot that the two men held between them. Renner brandished a club and the captives backed off, returning to their huddle in the corner.

Maria sat against the opposite wall. She watched the ground with a vacant expression, unable to muster any emotion towards the situation at hand.

"Back off! Or nun'ya gettin' this gruel," Patch thundered, making Maria flinch. He held up his side of the pot for emphasis. The contents sloshed over Renner's side and the man scowled as some spilled onto his shoes.

"Watch it, Patch! These are new boots."

"Ain't like it's gonna burn through your toes," Patch retorted. "Keep that club ready, in case any of 'em get weird ideas." He pointed a suspicious glare at Maria who was too tired to return it.

Renner and Patch placed the pot in the center of the

room, motioning for Correll to come over.

"You know how this works," Renner told him. "Make sure they all eat. Doesn't do us any good to catch folks if we try to sell them half-starved."

Correll nodded acknowledgment, keeping his head lowered and his shoulders hunched.

Renner turned to leave but something stopped him in his tracks.

He fixed Correll with a suspicious eye. "What happened to your cheek?"

Maria stiffened but Correll didn't miss a beat. "I scraped it on a rough patch of wood, is all," he replied. "I imagine it looks like a cougar got me with how much it's set to stinging. You wouldn't happen to have a rag I could use to wash it?"

Renner huffed. "Captain won't be happy. You're one of the better-looking ones. Don't do anything else to that pretty face until we're ready to sell you. 'less you want to end up on some remote farm that likes whipping their slaves for the fun of it."

Correll ducked his head again. "I do try not to waste the few gifts my ma left me."

"You comin'? I ain't waiting all day!" Patch called from the door.

With one last suspicious glance in Correll's direction, Renner left, locking the door behind him.

Maria let out the breath she'd been holding. Slumping against the wall, she watched as Correll organized the distribution of food.

He seemed to be a leader of some sort among the captives. He was levelheaded, strong and didn't let their situation hinder his optimism. He made sure that the children ate first, then the elders and finally, the rest of the captives. They had to take turns as Patch and Renner had only supplied them with two bowls.

Maria refused when food was offered, eyeing the greyish slop with disinterest.

"You'll need to eat something to keep your strength up," Correll told Maria. "If an opportunity to escape arises, you don't want to be caught unawares."

Andrea took her bowl without complaint and Maria's good sense won out. She choked down the food, trying not to gag as the lumpy paste hit her stomach.

As Maria ate, she considered the strange man before her. Correll's manner seemed to alternate between the talkative, nervous farmer that she had first met and the intense, serious man who had told her not to use her magic in front of the pirates. She assumed that the farmer facade was an act he was putting on for the pirates, but that just made Maria more curious about the other persona. What exactly was he hiding behind his mask of simplicity?

Maria's stomach roiled as she finished the last bite of the sludge, but she forced the food to stay down. She closed her eyes, leaning back against the wall.

CHAPTER SEVEN
Susanoo

Maria *awoke to something* cold and hard encircling her wrists. She bolted upright, chains jangling as she looked around wildly.

"Calm down." Andrea's voice made her jump.

Andrea was also chained, her wrists looking comically small in the large metal cuffs. She put a hand on Maria's shoulder reassuringly. Looking around, Maria saw that the other captives were in a similar predicament.

"They added the chains while you were sleeping," Andrea told her. "Apparently, we're almost to Gorena."

"So you do speak."

Maria stiffened as Captain Susanoo entered the room.

The Captain looked down her nose at them. "I did hope to have a word with you before we reached harbor. Patch, Renner."

At the unvoiced command, Patch and Renner grabbed Maria, Andrea and—to Maria's surprise—Correll. They dragged them up by their chains and followed the Captain as she marched out of the room.

The hallway was narrow and dark. The rough wood bit

into their bare feet and Andrea's shoulder brushed against Maria's as they walked. It was a wonder the whale-like brothers could even fit through such a cramped space.

They turned through a door and emerged into an office of some sort. A plain wooden chair sat behind the large desk in the center of the room. A small shelf was stacked high with rolled parchments that were crammed in so tightly that they didn't even rustle as the boat tilted this way and that. Susanoo took a seat in the chair and turned an appraising eye on the three of them.

Renner kicked the back of Maria's legs, causing her to fall painfully to her knees in front of the Captain. Patch did the same for Andrea and Correll.

"Now what to do with my newest stock?" Susanoo mused aloud. "You,"–she gestured at Maria–"the grumpy one, tell me more about yourself. What can you do? Do you have any skills? Give me something worth selling and maybe you and your sister won't end up in a brothel."

Maria glared at the Captain, hoping she would look defiant and not thoroughly terrified. Her heart beat so wildly that she was sure it could be heard by everyone in the small room.

The Captain nodded at Renner. The large man grabbed Maria's hair and yanked her head back painfully. She hissed through her teeth, biting back a shout. She didn't trust her voice at the moment.

"Well?" the Captain asked her. "I don't like being ignored. Stubbornness will only bring you discomfort."

"She can't talk!" Andrea burst out, drawing all eyes in the room. "She's not being stubborn, she just can't speak."

Captain Susanoo grimaced. "You brought me defective merchandise?" she demanded of Renner who was still holding Maria's hair.

Renner adjusted his grip nervously. "She screamed well enough in the forest. Her voice isn't easy on the ears but it's there."

The Captain narrowed her eyes at Andrea, "I don't tolerate lying." Turning back to Maria, she drawled, "This is hardly the situation for vanity. Say something or I'll have to punish your sister for her dishonesty."

Patch grabbed Andrea's shoulder and squeezed, drawing a sharp cry from the girl.

"Don't touch her!" Maria snapped.

Everyone in the room cringed. Correll's eyes widened for a brief moment before he returned to the nervous farmer facade. Renner released Maria's hair and she fell forward with the sudden release of pressure. She hit the ground hard, letting out a cry of pain as she collided with the floor.

The Captain cleared her throat. "I don't want you to open your mouth again. I'd sell a mute easier than whatever that was."

She turned her attention to Correll. "Now for you. I've had you in my possession for nearly a month now and you continue to insist that you've nothing to offer. I'm giving you one last chance. What is your skill set? What can I use to sell you to someone who'll treat you better than a disposable farmhand?"

Correll flicked a glance at Maria. He licked his lips, fixing the Captain with a look of uncertainty. "I'd be good as a farmhand, honestly. I was a farmer back home, you see. But I think the best thing I can do for you is help you sell them girls to a proper farm."

The Captain narrowed her eyes. "Explain."

"You might have trouble selling a mute, yes. But if you sell a set of three siblin's, odds are you could charge more for us and make 'em think they're getting a package deal."

The Captain tapped her fingernails on the desk. "You look nothing like the girls. Who's going to believe you're siblings?"

Correll shrugged. "Since when do siblings need to look like each other? If anyone asks just say I look like our da and they look like our ma."

She stopped tapping, leaning towards the farmer. "And the accent?"

"I'm actually quite good at accents," he said, matching Andrea's way of speaking perfectly. "I find my natural accent more comfortable, but I think I can keep this up long enough for you to sell us to the highest bidder."–Correll leaned in as he drove his point home–"Think about it. Two young women that are easy on the eyes and an experienced farm hand with some schooling under his belt. You have to admit that sounds like a more tempting proposition."

There was a moment of silence before a slow grin spread across Susanoo's face. "I knew I liked you. And not just because you're keeping the rest of my stock well fed. Very well, you teach the girls your cover story. If you double cross me, you'll find yourself working somewhere far less pleasant than a farm. The mines are always looking for new hands."

The threat hung in the air, meaning nothing to Maria, but the look on Correll's face—even if it was part of the act—told her it would not be an improvement on their current situation.

Patch and Renner returned them to their cell and Correll immediately went to work on explaining their new history. The story was complete with their parents' names, a farm they lived on, and a sickness that wiped out their entire town, forcing them to sell themselves into slavery to escape starvation. Maria listened with only half an ear. She watched the strange man who sat before her, trying to puzzle out what exactly he was getting out of this ridiculous charade.

Ask him why he's doing this.

Andrea didn't acknowledge the question visually, but she turned to Correll and repeated it aloud.

Correll massaged his temples. "I have my reasons, not least among them is the fact that you two won't last a day out there on your own. Follow my lead and I will keep you safe as long as I'm able. And for goodness' sake, no telepathy." The last sentence was barely a whisper.

Maria frowned. *How can you tell when I'm using telepathy?* she asked him, ensuring that Andrea could hear her too.

Correll sighed. "I assume there weren't many magic users on your island. Mages can feel magic being used. You two practically pulse with it. You're lucky that Susanoo only has one mage on this boat."

"The healer?" Andrea asked.

Correll looked at her sharply. "You've met him?"

Maria nodded slowly. She didn't like the look he was giving them.

He swore under his breath. "Then they may already know you're mages. We need to lay low and hope that Susanoo intends to hide that fact. She hasn't brought it up, so I think there's a good chance—"

Correll's words cut off as the door opened, admitting the healer that they had just been discussing.

Gray took in their little group with his usual sour expression. "Susanoo sent me to fix up your cheek," he said gruffly, stomping over to them.

The healer placed a glowing hand on Correll's cheek. He held it there longer than he should have needed. His eyes darted to Maria and he leaned in closer to their group, dropping his voice to a whisper.

"I don't have a lot of time here so I need you to listen closely. Susanoo doesn't know that you're mages and I won't be the one to tell her. I may have more freedom on this rotten boat, but I'm a slave here, same as you. I got a message out before we left last port so there should be someone waiting to get you out of there, but I can't make any guarantees. I've done what I can and you're on your own from here."

The man leveled one more look at Correll. He gave a slight bow of his head and left.

Maria watched as the door closed behind him. *What was that about?*

"That…" Correll began, frowning thoughtfully at the door. "…was a very good thing for us."

He turned his attention back to Maria, speaking so low that she barely heard the words. "Now, my mage talent isn't useful in this situation; my wits are all I can offer. So, I beg you, make my task a little easier. What magic are you using that it must be constantly maintained?"

Don't answer, Maria told Andrea, drawing an exasperated look from Correll.

Andrea hesitated. She dropped her voice to barely above a whisper. "We can't walk without magic. We're shifters and we need it just to get around. We would be much worse off if we had to drop the shift."

Correll narrowed his eyes, but nodded, acknowledging her statement. "Very well. But keep unnecessary magic to a minimum. The less conspicuous we are, the better."

Maria bit back a sardonic laugh. Inconspicuous wasn't exactly her strong suit.

CHAPTER EIGHT

Teldor

The port in Teldor bustled with activity as Maria and the rest of the slaves were led off of Susanoo's ship. Humans hurried this way and that on the crowded docks in a dizzying flurry of motion.

Maria stumbled as they were loaded into a covered vehicle. Correll gave her a funny look when she asked him what it was called, but he supplied the word anyway.

The few children in the group had to sit in their parents' laps in order to fit all the slaves inside the cramped wagon. Maria was squished shoulder to shoulder between Andrea and Correll. She kept her back to the wall and her knees pulled up to her chest, trying to take up as little room as possible.

Through the small barred window, she watched the humans as they passed, wrinkling their noses and hurrying on their way. Maria had grown used to the smell over the last few days. She must be contributing to it as well by now. She didn't care if the humans were put off by their stench; the less people who noticed them, the better.

As the wagon rolled to a stop, Maria steeled herself

for the reappearance of Patch and Renner. She was instead met with a tiny man who held a piece of parchment fastened to a board. Susanoo stood next to the man, watching him closely as he ran an appraising eye over the occupants of the wagon.

"Three children, nine adults," the man muttered to himself. "Not very good condition. Have you let them bathe at all?"

Susanoo gave him an unimpressed look.

The man sniffed, wrinkling his nose. "I suppose that's hard to do out at sea. No matter. Most of our clients won't bother bathing their slaves anyway. Are they all being sold individually?"

"The runts are with their mothers," Susanoo told him. "and those three are a sibling package."

The short man nodded, scribbling some notes on his parchment. "Alright, we'll take care of the sales for our usual commission. You can wait in the clerk's tent or you may return at sundown to collect payment."

The man turned back to the slaves as Susanoo walked away.

He tapped his quill on his chin, before nodding to himself. "Mothers first. You, you and you. Follow me."

The women followed, holding their children tight as a guard appeared beside the man.

The remaining captives were given food; a rock-like disk that Correll had called bread.

Maria did her best to force her teeth through the solid offering. After several unsuccessful tries, she snuck a surreptitious glance at the other captives. Ensuring that no one was looking her way, she quickly shifted her teeth back to normal and devoured the food as fast as she could.

Maria restored her human teeth, licking her lips. She looked up to find Correll's eyes on her. The almost imperceptible shake of his head brought color to Maria's cheeks.

She had never realized how much she relied on magic in her daily life until those past few days. Andrea was having similar trouble with the bread, but unlike Maria, she didn't attempt to cheat.

One by one, over the course of the day, slaves were led away from the wagon by armed guards. The small man didn't return after the first three women, apparently entrusting the transportation of slaves to the guards.

Maria fidgeted, keeping her attention firmly on the wagon door. She had the easiest job of the three of them—keeping her mouth shut and not using magic. She had already failed at the latter half of those instructions. Andrea was supposed to look pitiful to garner sympathy and Correll would do the talking if the need arose.

Her mind leapt to everything that could go wrong with this plan. What if she was forced to speak? What if she let her scales show and they were revealed as mages? What if she and Andrea were separated?

With a great deal of effort, Maria clamped down on her anxiety. What ifs would get her nowhere and she was in enough trouble without inviting more into her already chaotic situation. She straightened her shoulders and forced herself into stillness. When the guard returned for them, she didn't even flinch. The man ushered them out of the wagon, his sword glinting in the late afternoon sun.

The metal armor clinked noisily as they walked. The ill-fitting garments shifting on his shoulders in a way that must have been painful. Were slavers averse to providing good armor for a mere guard? Or perhaps he was new and hadn't had a chance to get his own set.

The guard turned down an alley that came to a dead-end. He turned to face them with a smirk.

Alarm bells rang in Maria's head. What was going on? Weren't they supposed to be going to the market? She took up a defensive stance, standing in front of Andrea. Correll did the same. Side by side, they faced the unknown attacker.

The man chuckled, reaching his hand into the satchel that he must have stashed at the end of the alley. Correll stiffened, but it wasn't a weapon that the man pulled out of the satchel; it was a bundle of cloth. He threw the clothes at Correll and then two more sets to Maria and Andrea.

"I wasn't told there'd be three of you, so you'll have to make do with what I have on hand," the man said, walking past them to the alley's entrance and glancing around as if checking for pursuers. "We need to get you into less conspicuous clothing before we head to port. You'll stick out like a sore thumb in the rags you got on now." He pulled out a key from the inner pocket of his coat and removed their chains.

Correll's posture didn't relax as he rubbed his wrists. "Who are you?" he demanded.

The man smiled. "A friend of Milano's. He's had me watching the port for weeks. Was getting ready to call it quits when you all docked right in front of me." The man shook his head. "You got the gods' luck with you, Highness."

The last word sounded like a title of some sort. She turned to ask Correll about it but he was already changing into the new clothes.

"Get changed, you two! We have to get to port before they organize a search."

The two men turned their backs to give Maria and Andrea as much privacy as was possible in the narrow alley. Maria quickly donned the clothing she was offered. The shirt was too large and the pants had to be tied at the waist to stay up, but it was better than the filthy rags that she had been wearing a few minutes prior. Andrea's outfit was much the same. Correll wore a long blue shirt that matched his eye color and a well-fitted pair of brown trousers.

He let out a contented sigh. "You don't know how long I've been stuck in that outfit," he told the new man. "You got word to Henry before coming to get us?"

The man nodded. "The Captain's waiting at port. He's been alternating between this one and Elyria's capital. He was set to cast off tomorrow morning."

Shouts rang out from the direction of the wagon.

"Time's up."

The man led them out of the alley and onto a back street. They wove around businesses and houses, keeping away from main roads and busy areas. Maria's heart raced along with her feet as she struggled to keep herself upright. She tried to copy Correll's way of running, but she was still clumsy on her unfamiliar legs.

Andrea stumbled and Maria's attempt to catch her sent them both tumbling to the ground in a tangle of limbs.

Correll was at their side in an instant, helping them up and pushing them forwards.

"I know you're tired, but we can't stop," he said breathlessly.

Correll stayed behind them as they ran, catching them whenever they tripped. The docks appeared ahead of them and Maria put on a burst of speed as shouts sounded from behind. She turned around to see men shoving their way through the crowd of people. Susanoo weaved in and out of view, her face bright red with rage.

The ground beneath them changed from dirt to wood and the pounding of their feet could be heard even above the shouts and the crowd. Maria kept her gaze locked on the ocean and their path to freedom.

They were almost there.

Correll shouted a warning just moments before pain flared near Maria's hip. She stumbled, catching herself and continuing on. She didn't stop to look at what it was.

CHAPTER NINE

The Dawn's Redemption

"Maria!" *Andrea ran to* her as soon as Maria hit the deck.

Maria screamed as her landing jostled the object in her side. The high pitched wail ripped through the air around her.

Andrea put a hand on her shoulder. *Your voice.*

Maria gritted her teeth. It took effort to shift her voice back through the pain.

"I'll get her fixed up in a moment, but this is going to hurt. Put this between her teeth," an unfamiliar voice said.

Maria, open your mouth. Andrea's voice was frantic as she pressed leather against Maria's cheek.

Give me a moment, Maria said, drawing deep breaths through her nose. *I'm trying not to scream again.*

As soon as she trusted herself not to cry out, she nodded, letting Andrea force the strip of leather into her mouth.

She bit down hard, thankful that she was able to hold onto her shift. Mermaid teeth would have made short work of the small bit of leather.

"Alright. I'm going to pull out the arrow. Hold her still."

Maria had only a breath to wonder what an arrow was before the man yanked the object out of her side.

She spasmed, her back arching. The leather in her mouth wasn't able to completely muffle her scream as it tore through the damp air. The man placed a glowing hand on the wound in her side and the pain eased, leaving her to sag in relief against the cold wood beneath her.

"Almost done. You're doing great. Just a bit longer." The man kept up a steady stream of reassuring words as he completed his work.

Andrea held Maria's hand in a death grip, staring white faced at her wound. Maria squeezed her hand in return, trying to comfort her frightened sister.

"There. That should do it. She'll need rest and food, but she's out of danger now."

Maria smiled weakly. *I've had enough adventure. Can we go home now?*

"That could prove to be a problem," said a new voice from just out of Maria's line of sight.

Andrea helped Maria sit up so she could look at the man who had spoken. He was tall and he held himself with an air of authority. Next to him, Correll was sitting against the ship's railing, looking exhausted but uninjured.

"You gave us quite a scare," Correll said tiredly.

Just trying to keep things interesting, Maria joked. Her smile faded as her brain caught up to the other man's comment. *What do you mean by 'problem'?*

The man looked down at all of them and opted to sit rather than tower over the group.

His expression was serious. "I am told that your island is unnamed."

Maria nodded slowly.

"And you don't know what direction it is, how far it

might be from our current position, or any other identifying information?"

She nodded again, not liking where this was going.

"I'm afraid to say," he continued, his expression turning grim. "there are a great many islands within a two day sail from Teldor port. It could take you years to find the one on which you lived."

"So how do we find it?" Andrea asked the man.

"We don't," Correll said. Noticing Maria's frown, he rushed to add, "At least not yet. It would be an impossible task for the moment and far too dangerous within Gorena's borders in light of recent events."

"Susanoo!" Andrea said, drawing everyone's attention. "Susanoo should know where it is."

Correll looked incredulous. "You can't be suggesting we go have a chat with her."

Andrea blushed. "No… I just… never mind."

Maria searched her brain for some way to get home. They could find the village easily enough underwater. But could they manage to sneak off of the ship with so many humans around? She watched the two men for a long quiet moment.

We have nowhere else to go, she told them, a note of discouragement sneaking into the words.

Correll straightened. "I have already told you that I will protect you as long as I'm able. That is doubly so now that I have put you in this predicament. Follow me to Falareach, the capital of my country, and when this mess has died down, I will help you return to your island. You have my word."

Maria tried to keep her expression neutral. *The word of a farmer?*

The other man turned to Correll. "You haven't introduced yourself? In three days?"

"It wasn't as if I was using my real name," Correll

retorted. "I introduced myself with my usual cover story." He turned to Maria, an apologetic look on his face. "I'm afraid I haven't been honest with you. In Susanoo's clutches, I couldn't take any chances with my identity."

He stood, sweeping a stately bow with every ounce of the composure that he had been hiding over the past few days. "I give you my word as Crown Prince Damian of Falara. If it is within my power, I will see you returned safely to your home and kin."

Maria blinked. She couldn't have heard that correctly, right? She would have been less surprised if Correll—Damian, she supposed—had claimed to be a giant squid. Of all the people they could have run into mere hours after coming to the surface, they had been thrown into a dingy cell with a human prince? Were there more princes on the surface than in the under kingdoms, perhaps?

Andrea was not similarly tongue tied. "I thought princes were supposed to be dashing and… princely, I guess."

Maria hissed, smacking her sister.

"I'm just saying!" she said defensively, rubbing the sore spot on her shoulder. "He doesn't look much like the princes Mama used to talk about."

Maria rolled her eyes. *Mama never described a prince's looks, and I think he's proven himself sufficiently heroic. Now hush before you get us into more trouble.* Maria didn't include the Prince or the Captain in her telepathy.

Andrea looked sheepish, nodding her apology to the Prince. "Sorry," she mumbled.

Prince Damian chuckled. "Everyone is entitled to his or her opinion," he said. "Though you might consider a bit more discretion when dealing with royalty. My brother Aiden is not so relaxed."

She's normally more tactful, Maria lied. *Thank you for rescuing us.*

"We have the good Captain here to thank for that." The Prince gestured to the other man. "Allow me to introduce Captain Henry Milano of the king's vessel Dawn's Redemption."

I'm Maria, and this is my sister Andrea.

She turned to the man who had helped them out of Teldor, raising her eyebrows inquisitively.

"Anthony Hidgens," he supplied. "Freelancer and mercenary as needed."

"And I'm Kern."

Maria started, turning towards the sound of the voice. A small creature that she hadn't seen before was standing a few feet away. He looked very much like a human, except that he stood a mere three feet tall with large ears that stuck out to either side of his head.

He extended his hand toward Maria with a smile.

Maria had seen this once before when she had met the Prince. She extended her hand in the same fashion, hoping she was doing it right.

The small man grabbed her hand and started shaking it up and down. "Ship's healer," he continued his introduction. "I'm a winderling and we're good at that sort of thing. I do think you should get some rest. Magical healings can be quite taxing on the body, especially for shifters. Your bodies never know what form you're supposed to be in."

Maria grew curious. *Are there many mages with a shifting ability?* she asked as he let go of her hand.

"They're common enough across several species," he said cheerfully. "You won't find a winderling shifting—we like to stay the way we are—but I've heard of elves with the ability. Centaurs, too."

"What's an elf?" Andrea asked, leaning closer to the small healer.

Kern looked taken aback. "You don't know what an

elf is?"

Our island is fairly isolated, Maria said.

The winderling nodded. "Well, elves are like humans with pointy ears and haughty temperaments. Not that humans can't be haughty, but it does seem to be genetic where elves are concerned. As for Centaurs—you haven't heard of them either, yes? Right. Centaurs are similar to horses, but they have the upper body of a human. Terrible sense of where they're standing. The amount of times I was almost squashed by a centaur's hooves!"

Maria frowned. *Horses?*

Kern's eyes widened. "You *were* isolated! Horses are—"

"I think there's plenty of time to tell Maria and Andrea about life on the mainland," Prince Damian interrupted in an amused voice. "but I believe you were saying that Maria should get some sleep."

"Right!" Kern rushed to show Maria to a room on the bottom level of the boat.

Several beds lined each wall and Maria sank into the nearest unoccupied one. Andrea followed her into it, rather than claiming one for herself. Maria snuggled close to her sister as she drifted off to sleep.

~~ * * * ~~

Maria awoke to the sound of steady breathing. Every bed in the little cabin was full, and the occasional snore echoed off the low ceiling.

She shifted her eyes back to normal so she could see clearly in the dark room as the boat rocked gently back and forth with the ocean swells. She nudged Andrea awake, shushing her when she grumbled about the hour.

We need to come up with a plan, Maria told her urgently. *We can't just follow them to Falareach.*

Andrea yawned. *Why not?*

Maria gaped at her. She couldn't be serious. *Why not? Because they're humans. Because we're not. Because humans do bad things to things that aren't human.*

Andrea raised an eyebrow. *Mama was human.*

Mama is the one who warned us to stay away, remember? Maria shook her head. *We need to get off of this boat. If we can get in the water, we can find a settlement and get directions back to our village.*

Andrea propped herself up on her elbows. *Or we can stay here and not get eaten by sharks in a deserted patch of the ocean. What makes you think there's a settlement within a hundred leagues of here?*

It's better than following an unknown prince to an unknown country and getting discovered as mermaids the moment one of our magic slips, Maria countered.

Andrea frowned uncertainly. *Fine. How do we get off this boat?*

Follow me and stay quiet.

Maria slid off the bed. She kept an eye on the sleeping sailors as she snuck over to the door, Andrea following silently behind. The creaking of the door's hinges sounded like thunder in the relative quiet, but no one stirred. She breathed a sigh of relief and slipped quietly into the hallway, closing the door behind them.

Once on the upper level, Maria looked around to make sure that they were alone. The air was filled with the dull roar of waves crashing against the side of the ship. Only one sailor seemed to be awake; a man who sat in the lookout basket suspended in the air by a tall wooden pole. Maria carefully edged her way to the railing, keeping her attention on the sailor as she readied to hoist herself over and into the water.

"You're awake?"

CHAPTER TEN

Introductions

M_aria spun around at_ Prince Damian's voice. The man was standing at the rail just out of sight of Maria's original position.

She cursed silently, willing her face into a neutral expression. *It was stuffy in the cabin.*

Prince Damian chuckled. "Never liked it much myself. Though I think you'll find that there's not much to see out here in the dark."

He turned his face outward toward the sea. Maria followed his gaze, her mermaid eyes allowing her to see the world around them clearly. The ocean was dazzling in the dark. Rather than it's usual vibrant blue, as it would appear in full sunlight, the water shone a deep sapphire that pulsed with the energy of each mighty swell. Smaller pockets of movement created a texture to the landscape that sent moonlight bouncing in every direction. Her breath caught, She had never seen the ocean like this before.

Maria shifted her eyes back and had to work to keep the awe out of her voice. *Not much to see,* she agreed.

Andrea leaned over the railing to look at Prince Damian. "Why are you out here? I thought you were sleeping too."

Maria bit back a groan and pinched her sister. Andrea shot her a glare before turning back to the Prince.

Damian shrugged. "It was stuffy in the cabin," he replied with a wry grin. He sobered quickly, however. "It reminds me a bit too much of Susanoo's boat. Its cleaner and not as dank… but a bit too similar right now."

They fell silent. Maria watched the Prince as he stared into the darkness. She knew very little about the man in front of her. Everything he had told her thus far had been a lie. But that wasn't so different than what she was doing, so she was hardly in a position to judge.

Still, she couldn't help but be curious. What was his country like? And the humans? Neither the Prince or his companions had harmed them, even if that was due to ignorance more than acceptance. Maybe she could go just for a little while. It wasn't particularly difficult to hold her human form.

Maria felt a small stab of guilt at the thought. She turned out towards the ocean and contemplated their next move. They had failed to get into the water, but there would be another opportunity. If they waited until daylight, they could do some proper scouting to find the best place to sneak over the side. Then it was only a matter of finding a night that the Prince wasn't so restless.

As the sky began to lighten and the oppressive darkness of the ocean began to fade, the Prince shifted his gaze slightly upward.

A gentle smile touched his lips. "I've always loved sunrise," he said.

The horizon slowly blossomed into a vibrant orange, the ocean reflecting the hue and casting the world around them in a brilliant gold. Little accents of purple danced around in the water.

Andrea drew in a breath. "It's beautiful," she whispered reverently.

The Prince nodded. "Sunrise on land is gorgeous, but a sunrise at sea is truly a sight to behold."

All too soon the color faded and the ocean returned to its normal hue.

"Come with me," Prince Damian said abruptly, pushing himself away from the railing. "People will be rising soon and now is as good a time as any to introduce you to the crew. It's a long trip back to Falara so try not to get on anyone's bad side."

Maria tensed and the Prince laughed. "I'm teasing. Don't worry, they're all nice people."

To you maybe, Maria thought. *How would they act towards a half-mermaid?*

The Prince led them around, introducing Maria and Andrea to several sailors as they rose for the day. Most of the names went in one of Maria's ears and out the other. She wasn't planning on sticking around long enough to remember names anyway.

"You've already met Kern," the Prince said as they came up to the little winderling.

"Nice to see you again, Miss Maria, Miss Andrea," Kern said cheerfully.

It's nice to see you, too, Maria replied. *I haven't had the chance to thank you properly for saving my life.*

Kern waved a dismissive hand. "What kind of winderling would I be if I didn't help a traveler in need?"

Andrea shook her head, her face clearly showing her amusement. "I don't even know what a winderling is," she said.

Kern's eyes widened in horror. "You've never heard of a winderling?" Maria thought the little man might faint.

"They hadn't heard of elves, either," Prince Damian

reminded Kern.

"Well elves are standoffish and rude," Kern said in a tone that suggested that this should be an obvious distinction. "I wouldn't be surprised if people avoided them, but winderlings are quite personable, you know. Don't tell me there weren't any on the whole of your island!"

Maria shrugged. *It was a very small island.*

Kern harrumphed. "I would like to have a word with that winderling. Really! If he is hiding from the people he should be helping. Never heard of a winderling!" Kern continued to mutter to himself as he walked away.

"You'll get used to it," the Prince told them. "Kern is of the opinion that there is a winderling hiding behind every rock. I have only met one winderling and that is Kern himself. I assume the poor man just misses his people."

He led them down into the boat and to an office that looked a lot like Susanoo's. Only instead of a small bookshelf stuffed with parchments, this room had a wall full of books and several maps spread across a heavy wooden desk.

"Your Highness," the Captain greeted as they walked in. "I would've thought you'd still be sleeping."

"I slept fine on Susanoo's boat," he replied. "I've been introducing Maria and Andrea to the crew. I brought them here last so we could discuss plans for the future."

Maria shifted her weight uncomfortably. If she and Andrea succeeded in escaping then this conversation wouldn't have any bearing on the future. Still, she didn't like making promises that she didn't intend to keep.

"I was under the impression that they were following us to Falareach," the Captain said, raising an eyebrow.

"I do believe that is the case, but there is the problem of housing once they're there. I don't think that I can offer them the hospitality of the castle." The Prince looked embarrassed, an expression that Maria was not accustomed to seeing on the usually confident man's face. "I was wondering if you might know somewhere they can stay while I make arrangements."

"While you fight with your father, you mean." The Captain gave the Prince a knowing look. "I'm afraid I am not planning on staying long in port. But I do know of a few good inns that you could take them to. I shall have a list made up for you."

"Thank you." The Prince nodded. "Now that's out of the way, I wonder Maria, if you wouldn't mind demonstrating your mage ability for the Captain and I."

Maria took a step back, narrowing her eyes. *Why?*

The Prince held up a hand. "No one will force you. However, it is polite when traveling on a ship to inform the captain of your abilities, so he knows what to expect in case of emergencies. Especially when one's magic is…"– he touched his cheek where he had been scratched by her claws–"…of a more dangerous sort. Rest assured; you have already been given my word of protection so there will be no repercussions if you choose not to show us. We could hardly throw you into the ocean and leave you to drown."

Maria grimaced and the Prince's frown deepened. "We won't throw you off the boat," he assured her, misinterpreting the reason for her discomfort.

Andrea laughed. "You underestimate how much my sister loves the water!" she told them.

What are you doing? Maria hissed.

Trust me, Andrea told her privately before continuing aloud, "My sister and I are shifters, as you already know. We can only do partial shifts, though. I can't shift into an orca or anything like that."

Andrea shifted, bringing out her brilliant blue scales. She sparkled in the small office, drawing impressed looks from the Prince and the Captain. It was odd for Maria to see her sister in a form that was so similar to her own natural one.

It took Maria several breaths to realize that everyone in the room was looking at her.

Shift, Andrea prompted. *Just the scales. I've seen you do it loads of times.*

Not normally for an audience, Maria snapped back.

The two men waited expectantly, having been unable to hear the short exchange.

Maria took a deep breath. Closing her eyes, she let her scales ripple over her arms and legs, stopping at her collarbone. Gills formed on her neck and her eyes shifted into the slit pupils of a mermaid. She opened them, squinting as her eyes adjusted to the light.

The Prince looked down at her hands. "and the claws?"

Maria blushed, pulling out her claws and holding them up for inspection. *They're sharp enough to do damage, but I don't use them often.* It was true enough. She wasn't fast enough to catch her prey and had to rely on other merfolk for food. Just another one of her limitations.

Andrea shifted back to her human form and Maria followed suit.

Prince Damian turned to Andrea, a crease between his brows. "You told me that you can't walk without your magic. That shift…" He let the end of his sentence trail off.

Andrea looked down at the ground. "I'm… crippled," she said carefully. "An accident of birth. I'd rather not show it if that's alright."

"That's fine," Captain Milano interjected. "We're not interested in embarrassing you or prying into your private lives." He exchanged a look with the Prince, "Although," he continued more slowly. "there are healers back in Falara that specialize in birth defects. Perhaps after we reach port, you might like to visit–"

"No!" Maria said aloud, her screechy voice making the Captain cringe. She took a deep breath and switched back to telepathy. *I mean, that's not necessary. We can get along fine with our magic. It's not really something that can be fixed, in any case.* She didn't think that mixed parentage counted as a birth defect.

The Prince looked unconvinced. "Perhaps Kern could–"

Perhaps I could return to my bed, Maria cut him off, hoping to end the conversation. *I am still tired from the last few days and would benefit from a few extra hours of sleep, I think.*

Prince Damian watched her for a long moment. She bit the inside of her cheek, trying not to squirm under his intense gaze.

"Of course," he said, his voice clearly concerned. "Can you find your way back to the cabin?"

Yes, thank you. Maria hurried down the hall, trying several doors before she finally found the right one.

The assertion that she was tired had been an excuse, but it hadn't been a lie. As soon as Maria's head hit the pillow, she fell fast asleep.

CHAPTER ELEVEN
Jumping Ship

M_aria awoke disoriented, the_ whispered taunts of her dream still ringing in her ears. *Two-tailed freak. Half-monster. Land-fish.* The childish quality of the insults didn't do much to lessen their sting. Back in the village she had thought that, after she was grown and married—a proper wife and mother—the taunting would die down and she could truly be part of the community. She thought she might actually have friends and a place to belong.

Would she ever get the chance now?

Maria angrily wiped a tear from her face. Self-pity had never helped her in the past and it wouldn't help her now. What she needed was a task to distract herself until they could make their escape.

The only problem was: what was she supposed to do on a boat full of humans?

Men moved about on the deck, attending to various tasks that Maria had no name for. She stood there and watched for several minutes, unsure what to do. Andrea sat on a box by the railing, swinging her legs cheerfully as she watched the sailors go about their duties.

"You're awake!" Andrea jumped off the box and ran over to Maria, excitedly grabbing her arm. "I've been so bored!"

The last of Maria's gloom lifted as she smiled down at her sister.

You could have found some way to be useful, she teased. *Or else, you could have searched for a way off this boat.*

Andrea rolled her eyes. *Your confidence in me is touching,* she replied sarcastically. *As if I've been idle this whole time! I've been watching the humans to try to find a blind spot in their shifts. They seem pretty busy during the day. I think we'll have better luck at night.*

Maria leaned against the railing and nodded. *How long did I sleep?*

Several hours. You get the night shift for scouting. She nodded subtly at the other side of the deck. *You're going to want to keep an eye on the spot over by those crates. Might take some sneaking to get there, but it's a blind spot for the lookout.*

Maria raised her eyebrows. *And how do you know that?*

Andrea grinned broadly. *Did you know that basket is called a crows nest? I don't really know what that means, but you can see so far from up there! You should see it for yourself. I have never found myself jealous of a bird, but I just might try shifting into one someday.*

Maria shielded her eyes from the sun as she gazed up at the crows nest. She was quite confident that nothing, in the water or on land, could convince her to climb to such a height.

She shook her head. *I'm starving. Where can we get something to eat?*

~ ~ * * * ~ ~

Maria waited until she was sure that the men were all asleep before she snuck out from under the blankets. Andrea yawned, resettling herself under the covers.

Stay awake. Maria told her, *If we get a chance to run, we shouldn't hesitate.*

The deck was quiet except for the rhythmic crashing of the waves against the ship's hull. Maria shifted her eyes to see better in the low light. She scanned her surroundings, making sure this time to check the railing for any sign of the Prince. Only the man in the crow's nest was awake and his gaze was turned out to sea. Could he actually see anything in the abyssal landscape?

The coast looks clear. Come on.

Maria waited impatiently, keeping her gaze locked on the lookout, until Andrea appeared at her side several breaths later.

The two girls inched their way around the deck. They hugged the railing, staying low and out of sight. Maria didn't dare to breathe. As she crept forward, she kept an eye on the one man who could foil their escape. His gaze was turned away from them as he watched the inky black horizon.

Even as they slipped into the blind spot that Andrea had mentioned earlier, Maria didn't relax. Her heart pounded in her ears. She wiped her sweaty hands on her shirt and risked a glance over the railing.

How far down is it? Andrea asked nervously.

Maria grimaced, *Really far. But it's water. We should be fine.*

Should we wait until tomorrow? We can get a better idea—

We can't wait, Maria cut her off. *If we wait too much longer, we won't be anywhere near the village. We don't know where Falara is in terms of the under kingdoms. What if we end up in hostile territory?*

What's more: Maria would lose her nerve if they waited too much longer. Even now the idea of slipping back into bed and leaving their problems for another night was dangerously appealing.

Maria took a deep breath. *I'll go first.*

She launched herself from the railing, steeling herself for the icy cold of the ocean. The few seconds to the water's surface felt like an eternity.

Maria hit the water with a painful crunch. Her vision blurred as pain blossomed in her left ankle and she let out an involuntary cry.

"Maria!" Andrea's scream rang out over the crashing of the ocean, catching the attention of the lookout.

"Man overboard!" the man bellowed, his voice carrying easily across the distance to Maria. Within moments, several men were running across the deck.

Maria cursed. *Come on! We have to go now!*

Andrea hesitated, her eyes wide. *That sounded like it hurt,* she said nervously, wasting precious moments.

I'm fine. Maria grit her teeth. *Make sure you don't go in at an angle. The water is harder than I was expecting.*

Andrea placed her hands on the rail but it was too late. Prince Damian appeared and dragged her away from the edge. He held out two hands toward Maria as if trying the drag her from the sea with invisible strings.

Maria felt the water around her stir. She thrashed wildly as she rose into the air. Frustration coursed through her, accompanied by the steady throbbing of her ankle.

Try to stay still. The Prince's telepathic voice was strained with effort. *It's difficult to move this much water as it is.*

Maria fell limp, allowing herself to slip fully into the bubble as she waited for the Prince to drag her back to the boat. They had been so close. Just a few moments more and they would have been racing away, too fast for the

Prince's magic to catch them.

No! Keep your head out of the water!

The bubble around Maria compressed, trying to squeeze her back out of the water. It pressed painfully on her injured ankle and she curled herself into a ball.

Stop that! she growled at the Prince. *I'm a shifter, remember? I made myself gills. The pressure is hurting my ankle.*

The squeezing sensation stopped and Maria sighed, trying not to wallow in self pity. They might not get another chance to escape, but at least Andrea hadn't been injured in the attempt.

Maria's stomach lurched as the Prince released his magic. She crashed onto the deck, water splashing in every direction. Uncurling, she got a good look at her ankle. It was twice the size it should have been and it was turning an angry shade of purple.

Maria! Andrea wrapped her in a hug. *Are you alright?*

Maria pulled away. Andrea's eyes were bright with tears and her whole body was trembling.

I was so scared, she sobbed. *I thought… I didn't know… I didn't mean to…* She seemed unable to finish a sentence, each abandoned statement punctuated by a shuddering breath.

Maria pulled her back into another hug. *It's alright,* she soothed, ignoring the throbbing in her ankle. *It was a stupid plan. You were right. We should have waited and gathered more information. There were too many unknown variables.*

Andrea sniffed, pressing her face into Maria's shoulder. *I thought you were going to leave without me.*

Never, Maria said, squeezing her tighter. *We're sisters. We stick together.*

~ ~ * * * ~ ~

Maria sat on her cot, trying not to wince when the winderling touched her swollen ankle.

Kern clucked his tongue as he examined the injury. "It's definitely broken," he said. "There's not much I can do for this. I'll splint it and wrap it tight, but you'll have to see a human healer when you get to Falareach."

"But you healed the arrow wound just fine," Andrea protested. "How can a broken ankle be worse than something that nearly killed her?"

Kern shook his head, putting up a finger to correct her. "Not worse. Different. I don't work with bones. Some winderlings might feel comfortable with such a risky venture, but I refuse. All those pointy pieces have to be set just so or you risk crippling your patient! No. It's safer to let a bone break heal on it's own than to try to force it back together with magic."

Andrea's brows knit together. "But you said seek out a healer when we get to Falareach."

"A *human* healer." He emphasized the second word. "Very different type of magic. Doesn't need thinking to heal with human magic. Less chance of failure."

Andrea didn't look any more enlightened by this explanation than Maria felt. She frowned down at the injury.

Maria sighed. *You don't have to look like I'm dying,* she told her sister, allowing her telepathy to travel to the whole room. *It's not like it's the first time I've been injured.*

Andrea grinned. "Like that time you met the wrong end of a stingray?"

Maria winced. *Don't remind me. I thought father was going to flay me. In my defense, it was really close to the village.*

Prince Damian looked intrigued. "One of these days I would like to hear more about your harrowing childhood adventures."

Maria chuckled. *It was actually a fairly boring child-*

hood. Only a few… eventful hiccups.

Captain Milano burst through the door. "What happened? I woke up to shouts of 'man overboard'." He took in Maria's ankle and her soaked appearance. "Don't tell me someone actually threw you off the boat."

Maria waved her hands quickly. *No, no. Nothing like that,* she assured him. *I couldn't sleep so I went to the deck for some fresh air. I guess I leaned a little too far over the edge. Next thing I knew, I was in the water and Prince Damian was pulling me out.* Maria's blush was genuine. The Prince's face softened and the Captain let out an exasperated sigh.

"Lance said that if Miss Andrea hadn't called out, he wouldn't have seen you down there. It could have been hours before we realized you were gone. Please be more careful in the future." He turned his attention on the healer. "How bad is the ankle?"

"Just finishing the wrapping. She'll want to keep off her feet as much as possible. Don't want to undo any of the good that her body will be doing. I'm ordering strict bed rest until we get to port."

Maria grimaced. *Can't I just shift it better? While I'm waiting to get to port, I mean.*

Kern produced a long stick out of thin air and whacked her on the head with it. "You shifters have no common sense! You stay in the form you were when you injured the ankle. The body is having enough trouble healing the injury without you confusing it with anatomical shifts. If you make it think it's already done it's job, it will stop working entirely, leaving you crippled until you can see a healer to put it right."

Maria's heart sank. There would be no escaping the boat before they reached Falareach. She couldn't sneak around with everyone on high alert and she couldn't survive in the water without shifting. How long will it take to heal?

Kern shrugged. "I don't tend to work the slow way. Two months, perhaps? We'll arrive in port long before it can fix itself."

Both Kern and Captain Milano left.

Mara didn't look at Andrea as she said privately, *We'll have to escape from Falara. I won't get far without a healer and it won't do us any good to escape if we hurt ourselves on the way down.*

At least we'll get to see more of the surface, Andrea said cheerfully.

Maria had to admit some level of curiosity as well.

Prince Damian cleared his throat, drawing both of their attention. "Since I am the one who dragged you onto this boat, I am responsible for you. Please be more careful. Tonight was… concerning."

He turned sharply and walked out, leaving Maria and Andrea in confused silence.

~~ * * * ~~

The rest of the trip was uneventful. Stuck on her cot for the entire week, Maria didn't see much of the Prince during the day. Andrea had seen him holed up in the Captain's office, discussing who-knows-what. Maria was more focused on her injured ankle, which had taken to itching over the past few days, and she distracted herself from the discomfort by planning their next escape attempt with Andrea.

If Falareach's port is anything like Teldor's, then there should be plenty of places that we can slip away unseen, Andrea said optimistically. *After your ankle is better, we just have to wait for the Prince to leave us at the inn and we can head straight to the water.*

Maria frowned uncertainly. *We don't know what mer-folk are down there, though. Or other sea-life for that mat-*

ter...

Andrea threw her hands up into the air. *We go or we don't. We've been swimming around in circles all week. If we're not going to make a decision, then we might as well wait and see what happens.*

Maria sighed. *You might actually be right about that. We can't do anything until we have more information. I just want to be ready when the time comes.*

Andrea was quiet for a long moment. *Why are we trying so hard to escape again?*

Maria blinked. *What's that supposed to mean?*

Andrea fidgeted with the blankets. *I just mean... everyone here has been so nice. Do we really have to leave? I bet we could find a place for ourselves among the humans. We could be normal for once.*

Only it's a lie. What happens when we're caught? The truth always comes out sooner or later.

Andrea nodded reluctantly. *You're right. I just wish...* She didn't finish her sentence.

Maria was glad she hadn't. This wasn't the time for what ifs and impossible dreams. They would wait until her ankle was fixed and the Prince was gone. Then they would come up with a plan to get home.

CHAPTER TWELVE

Calendula's Apothecary

T_he port in Falareach_ turned out to be much larger than Teldor, a fact that proved itself to be a hindrance to their original plan. Rows upon rows of boats lined the harbor, while still more floated in the surrounding sea. Men loaded and offloaded cargo from ships as children wove their way through the crowded docks. With so many boats and people, they wouldn't have a chance to slip away unseen. And even if they did make it into the crystal clear water, they would be spotted immediately, either revealed as mermaids or 'saved' by some well-meaning dock worker.

The only bright side was that Maria was no longer worried about hostile merfolk. There would be no way to hide in this patch of the ocean. Likely, the local merfolk had moved away long before the Falarans began sailing their waters.

Maria leaned on the Prince for support as they moved through the crowd, trying not to put too much weight on her ankle. She had objected to this arrangement, not wanting to inconvenience the man who had already done so much for her and her sister. However, since the Prince was the only one who accompanied them off the boat, there was no one else she could lean on.

Maria had inquired about the swiftness of Captain Milano's departure, but the Prince had merely shrugged and changed the subject. It didn't matter, she supposed. She would never see the Captain again.

Andrea had no trouble getting around on land. She dodged through the crowd like a native, checking out vendor stalls and shops as they passed. Her energy was infectious and Maria smiled despite herself, shaking her head in sisterly disapproval as Andrea came upon yet another food stall.

She says it's made with seaweed! she called back to Maria.

We don't have any money, Maria reminded her. *We don't even know what the currency is here.*

Maria could see the disappointed slump of Andrea's shoulders even across the several yards that separated them. Her sister said something to the shop owner who leaned in conspiratorially. Before Maria could object, Andrea was skipping back to her with three small wooden bowls.

What did you say to her? Maria demanded, accepting the bowl from her sister. The contents were a salad made of seaweed. It didn't look all that different from the fare back home.

"She asked where I was from." Andrea took a large bite of her salad, humming in appreciation. "I told her that we were from an island and this was my first time on the mainland. She said she was from an island too and she hoped we enjoyed our time here."

Maria shook her head. *One of these days that natural appeal of your's is going to turn on you.*

Andrea looked smug. "I can't help it if I'm cute."

Maria took a bite of the salad, surprised to find it sweet instead of salty. The seaweed had been smothered in a thick golden substance and sprinkled with seeds.

What is this? she asked the Prince, who already finished his portion.

"Honey seaweed," he replied. "It's a staple on the Azure Isle. This is an excellent example of the dish."

Andrea smiled. "Hurry up and finish so I can give the woman her bowls back. There's another store I want to look at!"

Maria hobbled along next to the Prince as her sister sweet talked treats from nearly every vendor they passed.

You're going to get lost! Maria chided. *At least stay within eyesight.*

Andrea giggled, returning to Maria's side. "Actually, you and Damian are easy to pick out! I see what he was saying about feeling power now." She wrinkled her nose. "It feels kind of itchy."

Maria would have described the sensation as ticklish. It grew stronger if she focused on it.

Maria stumbled over an uneven stone on the path, wincing as she put too much weight on her injured ankle.

That's Prince *Damian,* she reminded her sister, gritting her teeth.

Andrea rolled her eyes. "You and *Prince* Damian are easy to pick out," she corrected with a dramatic emphasis on the Prince's title.

The Prince chuckled. "Call me Damian if you'd like. I've never cared much for formality."

Andrea shot her a triumphant look.

Damian frowned down at Maria's ankle, which she held above the ground as she waited for the pain to subside. "We'll reach the healer soon. Think you can still walk? I could carry you if you need."

Maria's ears burned. *I'm fine,* she mumbled telepathically, starting to walk again with visible effort.

Damian's frown deepened, but to her relief, he didn't insist.

~~ * * * ~~

The little bell over the door rang as they entered the healer's shop.

"I'll be with you in a moment!" a cheerful voice called from behind a curtain that separated the front and back of the store.

The sign on the front of the shop read 'Calendula's Apothecary' with a pestle and mortar placed between the words. Fragrant plants lined the walls and bottles of liquid in every color of the rainbow covered every surface in the shop. Maria remained close to the door, afraid she might send something crashing to the ground and have to beg the Prince's financial intervention.

Andrea tilted her head as she examined a nearby shelf of remedies. "I thought this was a magical healer's shop," she remarked. "It looks more like a regular healer."

"That is an excellent observation," said a portly gentleman as he emerged from the back of the store. "The reason being, of course, a matter of practicality. I can only heal so many people before I am left exhausted. The apothecary shop allows me to create remedies for those people who don't need a full magical healing." The man nodded at Maria. "Although I can see you don't fall into that category. If you'll follow me, I can take a look at that ankle. How long ago was it broken?"

Andrea's eyes widened. "How did you know it was a broken ankle?" she asked him in an awed voice.

The cheerful healer chuckled. "Healing is my talent, my dear. I'm not fit for the palace, mind you, but I would be a poor healer indeed, if I couldn't diagnose something so painfully obvious, if you'll excuse the wordplay."

Maria grimaced briefly before smiling at the healer. *Any distraction from my ankle is welcome, even if the joke is at my expense.*

They followed the gentleman into the back of the shop, where he gestured for Maria to take a seat on a small cot that was set against one wall.

"Laughter is indeed good medicine, but a healer's touch never hurt."

He unwrapped Maria's ankle as Damian answered his earlier question. "She broke it a week ago, falling off of our vessel. The ship's healer is a winderling and didn't wish to work on a break. He advised we see a human healer as soon as we reach port."

The healer nodded his head knowingly. "Winderlings can be finicky. I met one once who refused to heal on rainy days. She said that the moisture in the air threw off her magic. Nevertheless, the first aid was carried out properly. Though I imagine it's quite painful. One moment…"

The man placed a gentle hand on Maria's ankle. His glowing palm brought with it a blessed numbness. She sagged, a soft sigh of relief escaping her mouth.

Andrea watched the healer work with interest. "Did you heal her? Just like that?"

The healer let out a startled laugh. "Oh heavens, no! It will take me some time to actually heal the break in her bones. I relieved the pain so she could sit more comfortably while I work."

Damian considered the man, his eyebrows drawn together slightly. "I thought you said you weren't fit for palace work. That skill alone should have won you a position in the healer's wing. Pain relief is not a common gift."

The healer lost his cheerful countenance. "Ah, well… truth be told, I had an unfortunate run in with the Prince. It was… illuminating." His smile returned, this time more forced. "But the city has plenty of use for my skills and I am doing good work here. Not everyone who needs heal-ing has the coin to see it done. That's where I come in."

Damian frowned, but he let the matter drop. "How long do you think the healing will take? We've just arrived from a rather long journey and I would like to get to the inn before nightfall."

"Oh, it shouldn't take long," the healer said. "I should have you out of here by lunch time."

~ ~ * * * ~ ~

True to his word, the healer finished around midday. Maria stood up and bounced a little, testing her ankle's ability to hold her weight.

She smiled broadly and turned to the healer. *So I can shift again? It won't cause any problems?*

The man returned her smile, looking more tired than he had when they arrived. "I assume you're referring to the mage ability? Yes, that should be alright. Nothing too drastic for the first few hours, mind you. Allow your body some time to adjust to being whole again."

Maria nodded. *I can only do minor shifts,* she told him, revealing scales from her knee to her ankle.

The man leaned forward, kneeling by Maria's leg to get a closer look. "Fascinating! Are those fish scales or reptilian?"

Andrea tilted her head. "Is there a difference?" she asked, moving closer so she could also examine Maria's leg.

Maria stifled a laugh. As if Andrea hadn't seen her leg a million times already.

"See here,"—he pointed to a line of scales on Maria's calf—"See how they're all separate? A reptile's scales are all connected. What's the range of your shifting?"

Mostly just this, Maria replied. *I was trying to mimic a fish tail so I could swim faster but it never quite works.*

He nodded. "My sister was a shifter, so I've seen some of her attempts to mimic animals she wasn't suited for. Perhaps you'd be better suited to land mammals. Though these are excellent."

Maria shook her head. *I'm just weak, is all. Our mother was a mage, but our father wasn't so our abilities are only half of what they should be.*

Damian laughed aloud. "If that were how it worked, I would be very weak indeed, as I inherited my magic from my great-grandmother. An eighth of my lineage."

The healer nodded. "My grandmother was the healer in the family before me. My sister inherited shifting from our father. Your parentage is certainly not the issue."

Andrea shrugged. "Maybe our magic is just broken. It takes me months to learn a new form, and Maria isn't even able to fix her voice box."

Andrea, Maria warned, watching the two men for their reactions.

Damian didn't even react, perhaps because he had already heard Maria speaking and thus knew what Andrea was referring to.

The healer, however, stood and reached his hands towards Maria. "May I?"

Maria shied away. *It's really alright,* she said. *I don't need my voice. I can use telepathy.*

The healer paused, his arms hanging in midair. "Is it not exhausting to use magic constantly?" he asked. "If I can fix your voice, that's one thing less for you to manage."

Maria waved her hand dismissively. *It's not like I'm using all that much magic. Just a few tweaks here and there.*

Andrea joined the two men in staring at Maria. She fidgeted under their scrutiny. Had she said something wrong?

Damian raised an eyebrow. "If that's what you call a little bit of magic, I'd like to see what you look like when you're making an effort."

Maria turned to Andrea. *You're using just as much magic as I am. You're not tired, right?*

Andrea glanced at the two men, biting her lip. "No, I'm fine. Maybe it just feels like a lot to mage senses."

Maria knew her sister well enough to know when she was lying.

We're going to the water. Right now. She grabbed Andrea's hand and pulled her out of the apothecary shop.

Andrea dug in her heels, throwing her weight back to try to slow their progress. "I'm fine, honest!" she objected. Then switching to telepathy, *What are you going to do, shift in front of the Prince? Are you planning on throwing everything away just because I'm a little tired?*

Maria turned on her sister. *And if you shift in front of everyone because of magic exhaustion?*

Andrea took a deep breath. *If it gets that bad, I promise I'll tell you. I'm used to this, remember? I had to use my magic constantly back home.*

Maria wasn't convinced. Her sister had a long track record of pretending everything was fine no matter how bad things got. Just look at her attitude after being kidnapped and dragged across the ocean!

Fine, Maria relented, releasing Andrea's hand. *But we find a way to get in the water as soon as the Prince is gone.*

Andrea agreed readily, looking more relieved than the situation seemed to warrant. This didn't reassure Maria.

Damian emerged from the shop and ran the short distance to where they were standing.

"Is everything alright?" he asked. "What was that about?"

Maria grimaced. *Sorry,* she said. *I overreacted.*

Damian's looked from Maria to Andrea. "I see," he said, though he clearly didn't. "We should head to the inn. They'll fill up if we wait until evening."

CHAPTER THIRTEEN

No Room at the Inn

The *he inn was two* stories tall with a space outside for animals and wagons. Several four-legged monsters stood there now, making odd noises as they munched on mouthfuls of grass. Andrea ran over to the animals, watching them with wide-eyed wonder.

"What's this?" she asked, putting a hand on the creatures neck. "It's soft, and its skin jumps when I touch it."

Andrea! Maria snapped. *Get away from that thing! It could be dangerous!*

Damian looked amused. "I believe Kern was going to tell you about horses but I interrupted."

"Ah," Andrea said, turning back to smile at the horse. "Horses are quite pretty."

Maria snorted. *If that's pretty, then I'm a dolphin,* she told her sister, taking in the giant skinny-legged beasts.

Their proportions were all wrong. The bulk of their body weight sat on four twigs that shouldn't have been able to keep them upright. Their heads were elongated and despite the fact that this animal had feet, they had no toes or claws. Instead, a round rock-like protrusion capped the end of each leg.

"You're just jealous that you'll never be as pretty as a horse *or* a dolphin," her sister teased.

Maria rolled her eyes. *You're ridiculous.*

The inside of the inn was overly warm. Every table was jammed full of customers and Maria struggled to hear herself think over the din.

Damian caught a server on her way to deliver a frothing beverage.

"I need a room for two," Damian told the woman. "and a hot meal if you're able."

The woman shook her head. "You won't find a room here, sir," she told him. "Nor any other inn in town. We're packed full of refugees from the latest attacks. If you're looking for a place to stay for you and your family, there's a refugee camp just outside the city walls." She walked away, leaving them standing in the middle of the crowded dining room.

Attacks? Andrea asked, using telepathy to be heard above all the noise.

Damian shook his head. *I've been gone for over a month now. I don't know of any attacks.* He glanced around the crowded interior. *Let's go see this refugee camp. Perhaps someone there will have answers.*

~ ~ * * * ~ ~

The refugee 'camp' consisted of three stretches of canvas propped up on poles for what shelter they might provide from rain and sun. The young and elderly were gathered under the largest one, while those refugees who couldn't find a space under the other two were spread out on the remaining grass. Nearly a hundred people filled the clearing outside the city walls, with bags under their eyes and hollow cheeks.

We're not staying here, are we? Andrea asked nervously. *I think I'd rather find someplace else to camp. Or we could sleep on the beach…*

Maria put a hand on her shoulder. *Relax. Once Damian leaves, we can go back to the water. We should be able to find a deserted patch far enough from shore to make our camp. Once we get our bearings, we can work on finding our way home.*

"What is this?" Damian demanded addressing one of the people running back and forth with supplies for the refugees. "Who is in charge?"

The man stopped just long enough to point to a small tent on the edge of camp before hurrying away to complete his task.

Maria followed Damian as he stomped over to the tent.

Inside, a man was frantically scrawling notes on a piece of parchment.

He didn't look up as they came in. "Jean, we need more blankets for the little ones. Go to the churches and see if they have any extra donations."

"You're in charge of this camp?" Damian demanded.

The man looked up, a tired crease to his brow. "I don't believe we've been introduced," he said slowly, putting his quill aside.

Damian straightened. "I am Crown Prince Damian." He paused a moment to let the words sink in. "Now tell me, are you in charge of this *camp*?" he emphasized the last word, as if it pained him to even call it that.

The man's expression melted into relief. "The crown has answered my request for aid?" he said, looking as if he might cry. "I had wondered if my messages were even getting through. I am Lord Henderson's eldest son, Sir Emri. I have been trying to organize this camp, but I don't have the proper manpower or funds to take in this many people at once."

Damian stopped short, confusion replacing his righteous indignation. "You've sent word to my brother?"

Sir Emri shook his head. "Last I heard your brother was on the edge of the kingdom to fight off the attacks."

"What's happened? What attacks?"

Sir Emri blinked. "You haven't heard of the monster attacks?"

"Monsters?" Andrea squeaked, ducking a little further behind Maria.

"Yes. The first attacks were centaurs, but I heard that elves and other magical beings have joined their ranks. It is a rebellion made up of most of the magical creatures in the kingdom."

Andrea frowned. "Magical creatures? I thought you said they were monsters."

The man gave her a level look. "Are they not?" he asked. "They burn forests and level villages." Sir Emri gestured outside. "Look around this camp. These are the people who have lost their homes—all of their possessions—because of this invasion, and they are the lucky ones. We had no forewarning."

"How long ago did this happen?" Damian leaned forward urgently, placing his hands on the table. "When was the first attack."

"About a month ago." Sir Emri sunk into a chair and placed his head in his hands, seemingly too tired to care to whom he spoke. "You're not here to aid my efforts, are you?"

Damian watched him silently for a moment. "No," he said in a regretful tone. "I have been… away… for a little over a month. I regret to say I was not aware of your situation. I will bring this matter to my father's attention as soon as I return to the palace."

The man's eyes snapped up to the Prince's face, his posture going rigid. "You haven't heard?" he asked in a measured voice.

Damian frowned. "Heard what?"

Sir Emri hesitated, as if choosing his next words carefully. "The King went with your brother to fight back the first wave of attacks," he said slowly. "He was felled by a centaur's arrow not long after. Your mother, Queen Helga, sits on the throne in his stead."

CHAPTER FOURTEEN
Now What?

D*amian froze, his eyes* locked on the man in front of him. No one in the tent seemed to breathe as they watched the Prince come to terms with the news. After what felt like several minutes of torturous silence, Damian donned an emotionless mask. He straightened, turning and striding out of the tent.

Andrea watched him go. "Um… are we supposed to follow?" she asked.

Maria exited the tent, spotting the Prince, who was already half way across the camp.

Prince Damian! she called.

He didn't look back at her. *You should stay here*, he said, unable to keep the emotion out of his mind voice. *I need to speak to my mother. I'll come back for you as soon as I'm able.*

Despite the circumstances of their unexpected good luck, Maria thanked the heavens for this most perfect opportunity. The Prince would no doubt take several days to return, plenty of time for them to slip away into the ocean. Or else, if luck was on their side, he may even forget to come back. The thought settled oddly sour in Maria's stomach.

Andrea came up beside her. *So, when do we leave?*

Maria thought it over as a line formed next to a table a short distance away. Volunteers ladled watery porridge into bowls and passed the food to the nearest refugee. Further down, refugees desperately grabbed a spot as early as they could. The small pot couldn't possibly stretch far enough to feed the ever growing line of people. Some of them would have to go without lunch. Maria's stomach growled, reminding her that she hadn't eaten anything since the honey seaweed several hours earlier.

It's none of our business, she thought, striding away from the depressing scene. *We're not even the same species.*

Andrea followed, pausing behind her when she stopped at the edge of camp. A few feet away, a mother knelt by her son, trying to get him to eat the meager offering she held.

"I know it's not very tasty," she said quietly. "But it will calm your tummy ache. Just a few bites, alright."

The boy sniffed, wiping his tears away with tiny hands balled into fists. His bottom lip jutted out as he nodded, opening his mouth obediently so the mother could feed him some of the food. He chewed briefly, his face screwing up in distaste, and swallowed with a dramatic gulp.

The mother smiled tiredly. "See? That wasn't so bad. Here, take another bite."

Maria didn't avert her gaze until the entire bowl was empty. The mother ran her hand over the child's hair.

As if feeling Maria's gaze on her, the woman looked up. "Did you girls get something to eat?" she asked in a concerned voice. "The food'll be gone before long."

Maria backed up a step. *We can take care of ourselves,* she told the woman. *We won't take food away from the refugees.*

The woman looked surprised. "You're mages?" she asked. "Are you not refugees then? Where do you live?"

Maria hesitated. *We don't live near here. It's complicated.*

The woman's face softened. "Isn't it always in times like these?" She beckoned them over with a hand. "Don't be stubborn. Go get something to eat before it's all gone."

Maria tried to argue, but the woman grabbed her arm and pulled her towards the food table.

"Linda," the serving woman greeted as they approached. "Another one of your strays? She has to get in line like everyone else." The woman's voice wasn't gruff, but she regarded Linda with friendly exasperation.

Linda smiled. "These girls are new so they missed lineup, can't they each have a half-portion? Come on, Dorris, they look half-starved!"

Dorris sighed, looking at the long line. "You know I can't," she said in a regretful tone. "Some of the folks at the back won't get food as it is."

"Linda!" an old man called from a tent nearby. "Bring 'em over. I'm feeling queasy, anyways. They can share my portion."

Linda dragged them over to the tent, grabbing an empty bowl on the way. "Jon, you're a gem!" she said, taking the bowl from him and spooning half of it into the empty dish, "Be sure to eat dinner, though. Queasiness is often hunger in disguise."

Jon scoffed. "And sometimes it's just queasiness. Don't go treating me like one of the children, I know you didn't eat this meal either."

"Oh hush!" She handed the food to Maria and her sister. "It's a bit cold and lumpy, but you'll get used to it. It helps if you're distracted. Why don't you tell me a little bit about yourselves while you eat?"

Maria stared down at the porridge, trying to make sense of the situation. These people had so little, why would they give food to a stranger? To her of all people? Was it because they thought she was one of them?

A small drop of water splashed into Maria's bowl. She hastily wiped at her cheeks, her brow furrowing. *Sorry, what? Oh, introductions. I'm Maria, this is Andrea.* She shoved a spoonful of food into her mouth. *We're not really refugees. We're not even Falaran. Our island is near Gorena. We haven't found a way back yet, but we don't plan on staying long.* She felt the need to make this clear, half-expecting Linda to yank the bowl out of her hands. When neither refugee said anything, she looked up.

Linda had a hand raised to her chest. "Gorena?" she asked incredulously. "But you're a mage! Surely you don't intend to go back there."

Jon nodded. "Seems to me you're just as much a refugee as any one of us. You've a place here as long as you need, don't you fret."

It was difficult to swallow, the tears forming a lump in Maria's throat. She forced the food down, placing the bowl in her lap. She couldn't accept the words at face value, none of these people knew that she wasn't human, but her heart hurt just hearing them. She wanted to believe them—to accept their hospitality and stay, even if just for a little while. But how could she? There wasn't space for two more people, nor was there food.

Maria stood abruptly, forgetting about the bowl on her lap. Porridge spilled all over the ground in front of her but she didn't give it a second glance. *We're going to talk to Sir Emri,* she told her sister. *I have an idea.*

~~ * * * ~~

I know how to fish, Maria said as she entered the main tent. *and I can gather seaweed and other edible plants. How much would you need to feed these people properly?*

Jon and Linda had followed them, as well as a few other curious refugees. They filled the opening of the tent, all eyes glued on Maria.

Sir Emri looked up from his notes, taking in the small procession. "You're a mage?" he asked incredulously.

Maria waved a hand. *That's not important. How much food do you need to feed this many people?*

"Far more than one girl can bring me, I'm afraid." He shook his head. "but every little bit helps. Karia!"

A young girl appeared at the door to the tent, her blond braids bouncing as she skipped inside.

"Take Miss…" Sir Emri looked at Maria expectantly.

Maria, she said with a nod of her head.

"Take Miss Maria to the shoreline. She says she can help with our food problem. Make sure you bring a basket or something this time. I'll not have more fish flopping around this camp."

"That was Dennis, I swear!" the girl objected.

Sir Emri pushed them all out of the tent without a response, returning to his work.

Karia turned to the group, hands on her hips. "Who's coming and who's staying?" she asked in an authoritative tone that made Linda chuckle.

"I'll leave them in your capable hands, Karia," the woman said. "Come get me if you need anything."

The group dispersed as Karia addressed Maria. "Maria, you said your name was? And this is?"

"I'm Andrea."

The girl nodded. "Nice to meet you! I'm the fusspot's niece. Got roped into all this against my will. Not that it isn't good work that needs doing, but I'm dying with all this running around and carrying things." She shook her arms out in front of her. "Ten year olds have little arms! What if they fall off!"

Andrea giggled. "Maybe they'll grow back," she suggested, drawing a giggle from Karia as well.

Contrary to the girls words, she seemed to be bursting with energy. She skipped as she led them away from the main tent. They stopped to grab several large cloth bags and a wheeled cart before heading to the shoreline.

"I still think this is too much," Karia complained as she pulled the cart behind her. "I bet you won't be able to fill even one bag, let alone enough to need a cart."

"We're mages, remember?" Andrea said with a laugh. "We have our methods. Don't go trying to peek, though. We don't want others to copy our genius." Andrea winked at the skeptical child.

"If you say so." Karia handed each of them a rough sack. "We better get a move on if we want to bring the fish back in time for dinner."

CHAPTER FIFTEEN

Gone Fishing

Maria *squinted out at* the ocean. The water was just as clear here as it had been at the docks. *We'll be back soon. Wait here.*

Maria ran into the water, Andrea right on her heels. She brought out her gills and scales, diving into the waves with an enthusiasm born of homesickness. The freezing water embraced her like a warm blanket and she breathed a sigh of relief, shifting back into her natural form.

I need to work on the mermaid voice, Andrea complained. *You get to express your joy freely while I'm stuck with telepathy.*

"And a tail," Maria added dryly. "Come on. I know you can fill these bags easily, but I want to get further from shore before you fix your tail."

The landscape underwater was familiar and different at the same time. Coral dotted the ocean floor and schools of fish darted about in the clear water. A tiger shark meandered lazily across the ground, scavenging for food as he went and a sea turtle circled Maria, playfully bumping into her. Maria smiled and ran her hand across the turtles back.

You're lagging behind! Andrea called back to her. *I don't even have my tail yet so you can't say I'm cheating.*

Maria laughed. "I can if I want to!" she said, racing after her sister.

When they reached a good spot, Andrea transformed, leaving her skin its natural state rather than bringing out her extra scales.

Andrea smiled. *It feels good to let go of the magic once and a while. Mama must have been perpetually exhausted.*

Maria shrugged. "I still don't know what you all are talking about. I haven't felt particularly tired since coming to the surface."

Andrea rolled her eyes. *We can't all be perfect.*

Maria guffawed. "There you go again with your ridiculous comments. Hurry up and gather some fish. I'm going to gather seaweed."

A grin spread across Andrea's face. *First one to fill their bag wins!* she said hurriedly before racing off into the water.

Maria laughed. "You know I can't win!" she objected, but she raced after Andrea anyway.

It took them about fifteen minutes to fill their sacks. They returned to the beach and a gaping Karia.

"You shouldn't have doubted two mages!" Andrea said haughtily.

Karia shook her head. "You were gone for an hour! How'd you stay underwater that long? I was watching. Neither of you came up for air."

Andrea put a finger to her lips. "Secrets," she told her.

Maria laughed at the way Karia's eyes bulged and she took pity on the girl. *We're shifters. Only little things, but gills are quite useful in the water.*

Understanding dawned on the girl's face and she grinned broadly. "Now if you'd told my uncle that, he wouldn't have been so skeptical! Load the bags into the cart and let's go. I can't wait to see the look on his face!"

"Shouldn't we go back out for more?" Andrea asked, pointing a thumb at the water. "We brought more bags."

Karia blinked. "You could get more? After swimming around for an hour?"

Andrea shrugged. "If it would help. I'm not too tired to go back out."

You just like being faster than me, Maria teased her privately.

A side benefit, I admit. But I really do think we should get as much as possible. It's less risky to do this all at once.

They filled six more bags, stacking the cart so high that it took all three of them to wheel it back to the refugee camp.

Sir Emri was turned away from them as he directed efforts to raise another tent.

"Uncle Emri! We got fish!"

The man didn't look their way. "Every little bit helps," he called, waving a hand. "Send it over to Dorris for dinner preparations."

The woman standing next to him tapped him on the shoulder and pointed in their direction.

Sir Emri's brows furrowed as his gaze followed her pointing finger. He gaped as his eyes landed on their massive haul.

Karia put her hands on her hips and lifted her chin proudly. "I think we managed a meal or two!" she said with a massive grin.

Andrea elbowed her. "You say that as if you helped," she teased.

Karia deflated. "I pulled the cart."

Maria smiled and ruffled the girl's hair, drawing a startled protest. *Don't listen to her, you helped plenty.*

Volunteers swarmed the cart, pulling bags of fish out and dragging them towards several large cooking fires. Dorris was yelling orders to people as they swiftly and efficiently prepared the fish for stew. One of the women took the cart from them, now laden with only the seaweed, and dragged it away.

"She's going to wash it in the stream," Karia explained. "Gotta get all that salt off before we turn it into something."

Within minutes several pots of stew were simmering over fires.

They're very organized, Maria remarked.

The girl shrugged. "We had fish stew almost daily for a couple weeks. Until we ran out of fish, that is, and the docks stopped sending donations our way. Leftover fish'll be put aside for tomorrow."

Sir Emri finished what he was doing and walked over to them, his expression full of gratitude.

"I can't thank you enough!" he told them. "How did you catch so many? Did you work with a boat?"

Karia beamed. "They're shifters! Brought gills right out of their necks! It was amazing!"

Maria blushed. *It was a coincidence that our skills were well suited for this task. I'm glad we could help.*

Emri shook his head. "I mean it, this was just what we needed. If we can keep people fed through food gathering, we can focus our funds on getting tents set up and other basic necessities." He hesitated. "Can you do this again? Or should we stretch this food as far as we can. I don't know how long—"

We can help, Maria cut him off. *We can't return home at the moment. As long as we're here, we'll do whatever we can.*

The man visibly sagged in relief and Maria knew she'd made the right decision. He thanked them again before moving away to organize the purchase of several tents and other supplies.

Andrea turned to Karia, excitedly. "So what should we do now? There has to be some other way we can help besides gathering food."

Karia shrugged. "Unless uncle gives me something to do, I normally just play in the field over there."

"You girls run along," Linda said, coming up beside them. "We've plenty of hands for this meal. Go take a much deserved break. Someone will call you when food's ready."

~~ * * * ~~

The field Karia mentioned was more like a overgrown patch of grass. Karia ran around the small space as Andrea chased her, both girls giggling as they played. Maria sat on the edge of the patch with her eyes closed, relishing in the cool breeze as it kissed her cheek. She had been so focused on their escape plan over the past week that she hadn't had the time to relax. Now that she had decided to stay a little longer, the future didn't seem so urgent. She layed down with a sigh and let her mind wander.

Working with the refugees was a risky detour, but one that felt right. They had the power to help these people even if the humans wouldn't help in return if they knew the truth. She thought of Linda and her little boy; of Jon who had given them the little bit of food he had; of Sir Emri who was doing everything he could to give them all a safe place to stay. Maria had never felt like she could be useful to anyone like that. But now she had a place to use her talents to help people.

How could she say no to that?

Maria felt a tap on her shoulder and she opened her eyes to see Linda's boy watching her nervously.

"Hello," the child said. "Thank you for the fish."

Maria smiled. *You're welcome.*

The boy gasped. "Mama!" He ran to Linda, who was standing a few feet away with her arms outstretched. "Mama! She talked in my head!"

Linda chuckled, scooping up the child. "They're mages, dear. That is a skill most mages have."

"Can I be a mage?" he asked excitedly as Linda walked back toward camp.

They had gone too far for Maria to catch the answer, but the smile never left the woman's face.

~~ * * * ~~

Many of the refugees came to thank them over the next few days. Maria put extra effort in remembering each of their names, feeling mildly guilty every time one of them slipped her mind.

Sir Emri approached them to work out a schedule for the fishing trips so he knew how long they needed each batch of food to last. After much debate, they decided on going out every other day.

With the food problem out of the way, Sir Emri focused his funds on acquiring tents for the refugees to sleep in and Maria helped set many of them up. She watched in satisfaction as every family was given a place to sleep that was covered and dry. A few of the individual refugees—those who had come without families—still had to sleep under the shelter of the large group tent. Some even chose to sleep under the open sky as a matter of preference.

"I'm not too young or old for sleeping on the ground," one man, Edmond, said when Maria had asked him why he turned down a tent. "If there's space after those that need it are settled in, then I might accept the offer. Besides, there's a beautiful light show in the sky every night. It'd be a shame to block it with a blank bit of canvas."

Several of the volunteers echoed his sentiment and

Maria had attempted to follow suit only to be met with universal opposition.

Linda sternly shook her head. "You're the reason we've food in our stomachs and a roof over our head. As long as you stay with us, you will sleep in a tent."

Maria blinked rapidly to clear her eyes. *Thank you.*

Linda placed a gentle hand on Maria's shoulder. "It's hard out in the world all by yourself. We're here for you and your sister. In difficult times, all we can do is come together and support each other until those times have passed."

CHAPTER SIXTEEN
Up In Smoke

W_ithin a few weeks,_ everyone who wanted one had a tent. No one fought for places in line because they never ran out of food. Even after the refugees increased—a consequence of word getting around that the camp conditions had improved—they managed to keep the food stores well stocked. They did require extra help on fishing days, but there was no shortage of volunteers for the task.

Karia insisted on coming every time they went to the water, saying that as the first person to lead them there, she had seniority and should never be excluded. Maria loved bringing the energetic child along. She even let her come into the ocean once or twice after securing permission from her uncle. They had to stay near the shore but she loved watching the girl's feet bob in the water while she gathered seaweed.

Some of the new refugees came from outside the city, fleeing their towns and villages on the outer edges of the kingdom. Others had come from Falareach, either coming from the streets where they had been sleeping or no longer able to pay for constant lodging at an inn.

As the group of refugees grew to two hundred, they were forced to set up a more structured command of the camp. Sir Emri slipped into the leadership role that he had already been fulfilling. He left Dorris in charge of the meals and assigned several volunteers under her to help with preparation and distribution. Linda was put in charge of organizing people; making sure that everyone stayed fed and that new refugees were given tents and bedrolls. The clearing outside of the castle was growing so cramped that some refugees chose to set up their tents just inside the tree line.

On days that they didn't go to the ocean to gather food, Maria and Andrea helped with chores around the camp. They spent most of their time cooking or cleaning up after meals. Many of the refugees objected to them having any chores at all, arguing that gathering food was more than enough contribution to the camp, but Maria refused to stop.

I like being useful, she told them. *and it isn't strenuous work. Don't worry.*

Following their example, many of the new refugees started picking up various chores as well, ensuring that the camp ran smoothly. Stomachs full and hands busy, the refugees settled into a routine that was surprisingly pleasant for such a bleak situation.

"So tell us again where you're from," Linda said as she scrubbed a pot in the nearby river.

The evening meal had finished quite some time ago, but as the refugees multiplied, so did the dishes. It was a great time for conversation, though, so Maria didn't mind that it took a while.

"An island near Gorena," Andrea replied as she rinsed the bowl she'd been cleaning. "We got stuck here because we don't know which one."

Sounds of sympathy echoed from the group of women

around them.

"Gorena's no place for a mage, in any case," Raina—one of the newer refugees—said. "Even the islands aren't safe with slaver's ships about. I had a cousin that was picked up by slavers. Never heard from him again."

From next to her, Karissa scoffed. "More like he just ran off with that pretty redhead o' his and never told you he was going." She dunked the dish she held into the water and resumed scrubbing.

Raina shook her head, pointing at Karissa with a wooden ladle. "I told you, I've talked to Amanda since. She's not seen him in years, she said."

Andrea shrugged. "Slaver's ship is actually how we ended up losing track of our island in the first place. They snatched us right out of the forest. What was the Captain's name? Soo? Sanoo?"

Susanoo, Maria supplied absently as she scrubbed a particularly stubborn grease stain.

The women all fell silent. Maria looked up to find them all staring at her and Andrea, eyes wide and mouths ajar.

"Susanoo?" Linda asked incredulously. "As in Captain Eliza Susanoo?"

I suppose, Maria said. *I only ever heard Susanoo, but I doubt there are many people running around with that name.*

Karissa whistled. "Never heard o' no one getting away from the Crimson Falcon before. How'd you give her the slip?"

Andrea glanced sidelong at Maria. *How much should we say?* she asked in a rare display of caution.

Keep the details vague, no need to complicate things.

The Prince hadn't returned yet—likely he never would—so there was no use bringing him up in conversation. As far as the refugees were concerned, the crown couldn't care less about them. Maria wondered briefly if they *should* bring the Prince up more, if only to show the refugees that the royals weren't all bad.

Andrea turned back to Karissa. "A kind gentleman recognized that we were mages and smuggled us out," she told her. "He left soon after we arrived, but he first showed my sister to a healer for a broken ankle and saw us safely to the refugee camp."

"Then we've him to thank for our good fortune," Linda said with a smile. "The camp was barely survivable before you two arrived, even with Sir Emri pouring all of his time and money into the effort."

Maria's cheeks warmed at the woman's praise. *I'm glad we could help.*

She wasn't used to getting compliments yet, but she was finding the phenomenon inspired a mixture of pride and embarrassment in her chest.

A scream tore through the air drawing all eyes in the direction of camp.

"That sounded like Sylvia!" one of the women said, worry filling her voice. They sat in tense silence, no one daring to move.

Other screams joined the first and the women abandoned their washing, running back to camp as fast as they could.

The scene was utter chaos. refugees tried to run away as men in steel armor grabbed them and dragged them to the side of the camp. They stood there in a large crowd, the children gathered in the center for protection. Maria scanned the area quickly, relieved to see that no one seemed too badly injured. A few of the refugees bled from head wounds and one clutched his arm to his chest, but as far as she could tell, no one was in danger of dying. Soldiers surrounded the refugees, holding them back as they tried to get back to their tents and belongings.

Tents that were on fire.

Men went through the camp with torches, setting every tent aflame as they passed. Refugees screamed and cried as the last things they owned turned to ash before their eyes. Maria raised her hand to shield her face from the heat of the growing inferno.

A soldier grabbed Linda's son and physically tossed him through the air at the refugees, drawing a shout of terror from the woman beside Maria. Jon caught the boy and held him protectively while he glared at the man.

Soldiers turned at the sound of Linda's scream, looking surprised but unconcerned by another group of refugees. They advanced on Maria and the group of women, brandishing swords in their direction.

Andrea scooped a rock from the ground and tossed it at the advancing soldiers. She missed her intended target, the rock falling to the ground a whole hands width in front of them. The rest of the women followed her example with much better aim. A few of the men who had neglected to wear helmets now regretted that decision as stones collided with foreheads and cheekbones. Stones clinked against armor, the heavier rocks drawing grunts of surprise. They didn't inflict any lasting damage, however, and the soldiers continued to advance.

The closest soldier ducked a stone and ran his sword along Maria's arm, drawing a long gash from her shoulder to elbow.

She screamed, her high pitched wail sending everyone to their knees, soldiers and refugees alike. Pain and anger made Maria lose her hold on her magic. Her vision shifted, taking in the fire with more vibrancy than her human eyes had allowed. Scales appeared on her skin and her fingernails grew into their usual deadly claws.

She grabbed the nearest soldier by the throat and dragged his face close to hers, baring her teeth.

The man stared back at her with wide eyes. "Please,"

he begged. "We were just following orders."

The field fell silent except for the roaring of the fire behind Maria. The other soldiers looked on in terror, her monstrous appearance bringing a complete halt to the attack.

Whose orders? she growled, tightening her grip.

The man swallowed against the pressure on his throat. "Crown Prince Damian."

The world froze, the sound of the refugees becoming distant and muffled to Maria's ears. She couldn't have heard correctly. The Prince had sent soldiers to destroy their camp? Why? What was the purpose?

The soldier slipped from her nerveless fingers, running away as soon as he regained his feet. None of the other soldiers seemed to have stuck around long enough to see if he was alright.

"Maria!" Andrea's scream cut through Maria's shock.

Maria reacted on instinct, whipping her hand out to grab the object that was coming down at her. She held the blade of a sword, the scales on her hand preventing any serious injury. She met the eyes of a boy no older than fourteen. He held the sword in a shaky grasp.

"Monster," he whispered in a shaky voice.

The word hit Maria harder than the sword ever could have. She stumbled backwards, her retreat halted by the flaming tents. The refugees all stared at her. She shifted back, scales pulling painfully on the gash as it reopened, bleeding freely on her upper arm.

Maria dropped into a defensive crouch, trying to look non-threatening without leaving herself open to attack.

Andrea appeared at her side, claws out and growling.

What are you doing? Maria hissed, swaying as she grew light headed.

Andrea ignored the question. "I'll flay the first person who touches her."

The boy who had attacked Maria dropped the sword and put his hands up, moving backwards until he stood with the rest of the refugees.

Maria shook her head, trying to clear it as she fell to her knee.

"We need bandages over here, now!" Linda yelled, running up to Maria's side.

None of the refugees moved. They watched Andrea warily, seemingly caught in indecision.

Linda glared at them all. "Gareth! Get your useless hide over here and give me a hand! Unless you want the person who just saved us all to bleed out while you stand there gawking."

The refugees snapped into motion. Gareth ran over, helping support Maria as they moved her away from the fire. Someone appeared with a bucket of water and some bandages.

The rest of the refugees did what they could to put out the fire. Running to the nearby stream and hauling buckets of water back with them.

Linda bandaged Maria's arm tightly. The bleeding seemed to have stopped but Maria didn't feel steady enough to stand. She sat there, watching the efforts of the refugees with a single question in her mind.

Why? She didn't direct the question to anyone in particular.

The refugees not currently occupied with trying to save the tents turned to look at her.

"Why what?" Linda asked, putting a gentle hand on Maria's shoulder.

Maria looked at her. *Why are you helping me? Helping us?*

Andrea was assisting with the efforts to save the refugee's belongings. Her blue scales shone in the sunlight, a subtle reminder that no one was to touch Maria.

Linda followed Maria's gaze and sighed. "I suppose you haven't had the most positive experiences with humans," she said. "but we're not all bad. We know the difference between magical folks who are attacking and those who are just trying to live their lives, same as us."

Maria shook her head. *You know the irony is, humans have been fairly good to me so far. It's my own people who have caused me the most pain.*

Linda tilted her head. "Is that why you left the ocean?"

Maria looked at her sharply.

The woman chuckled. "I know a mermaid when I see one. Though the partial transformation was a nice touch."

Maria opened her mouth and closed it again, unsure how to respond to such a revelation. The Falarans knew about merfolk? Or was it just Linda? Were there merfolk in the water after all? A million questions ran through her head but Linda continued before she could decide which one to ask.

"Whatever your past, you have a place here." Linda continued as she watched the fire with a sad expression. "We're all out here seeking a haven as the world crumbles around us. Human, merfolk or otherwise, we're safer if we stick together."

Epilogue

"W_e need to leave,"_ Linda declared to the group of refugees that had gathered outside the smoldering remains of the main tent.

Sir Emri had fled with Karia during the initial attack, along with more than half of the refugees that had taken residence in the small camp. The children were being looked after by the elders while the rest of them discussed what they were going to do next. That left about fifty people to join the meeting.

"Leave? and go where?" one of the men demanded. "We're already refugees! Are we to risk ourselves in the wild with monsters on the loose?"

Maria winced and Linda glared at the man.

"Look around you," she scoffed. "The crown burned everything we own! What protection do you expect to find here?" Her tone turned to one of warning. "And if I hear that word out of your mouth again, you won't be welcome in this camp."

A younger man agreed. "We'd all be locked up in jail cells if it weren't for Maria. They were fit to round us all up on that Prince's orders."

"If they didn't just kill us outright!" Karissa added. "I never thought Prince Damian would stoop so low!"

Maria was still conflicted over this new side of the Prince that she was seeing. It didn't add up. Damian had rescued them from Susanoo. He had brought them to Falara and made sure that Maria had seen a healer.

Then he left, Maria reminded herself, *he left you at a barely habitable refugee camp with no money and no way to get home.*

Andrea grabbed Maria's hand and squeezed it reassuringly. Maria shot her a small smile before turning back to the conversation.

"What about Hampton?" one of the women suggested. "I heard it's a ghost town nowadays. It has good strong walls and plenty of beds."

"And it's also on the edge of the kingdom!" another woman objected. "Not a two day's walk from the initial attacks."

"Maria can protect us," one of the younger women said.

Maria's eyes widened. "What?" she squeaked, her high-pitched voice making the crowd cringe.

Many of the refugees nodded their agreement.

"She sent those guards runnin' with just a couple'a words!"

"She can make us cringe just by opening her mouth! I bet the other mon—other magic folk'll be scared of her!"

"No," Linda said firmly. "Maria and her sister are welcome to come, but you will not lean your misguided hopes on the back of an eighteen-year-old girl who came to us for shelter. We survive as a group, we defend as a group, and we thrive as a group."

More heads nodded and Maria squared her shoulders.

I'm coming, she told the refugees before she had made

the conscious decision to do so.

Many of them looked relieved and Linda smiled warmly.

You all took us in. You made us feel welcome despite my… magic… Maria took a deep breath. *If we defend as a group, then I'll defend by your side.*

For the first time since leaving her village, Maria acknowledged the truth: There was no way for them to go home. They had no money for a boat, no idea which island was theirs and no idea which part of the sea they were in. In fact, she wasn't even sure if she wanted to go home. This wasn't just a risky detour as she had been telling herself for nearly a month. It was time for them to find a new path.

Are you alright with this? Maria belatedly asked her sister. *You don't have to come with me. You have a full tail, it's easier for you to find your way home than it would be for me.*

Andrea shook her head. *Not a chance,* she said, squeezing Maria's hand again. *We're sisters. We stick together.*

~ ~ END OF BOOK ONE ~ ~

About the Author

ADRIENNE MIONE likes to call herself a creative generalist, which is a fancy way of saying she's indecisively eclectic. Growing up in a highly creative family, she has picked up many hobbies over the years, from knitting to chainmail! When she's not writing you can often find her singing, drawing or playing an instrument (an occasion that may require earplugs). She also enjoys watching movies with her friends and family. From a young age, television was a beloved pastime in her family and it garnered a deep love of storytelling and all things fantasy. One day she hopes to have enough published books to fill a whole bookshelf with her works, but for now, she looks forward to each new release as her next great adventure.